Shared Lives,
Twin Sun

a novel

Anthony Garcia

Jornado de Exodo — Journey of Exodus

Shared Lives, Twin Sun
by Anthony Garcia

Books may be purchased in quantity and/or special sales by contacting the author or publisher at
xxicent@aol.com

Published by *Jornado de Exodo* — Journey of Exodus

Cover Art: Stevon Lucero, www.StevonLucero.com
Cover Art Concept: Anthony Garcia
Cosmic Drawings: Robert Maestas, www.RobertMaestas.com
Photography: Michael Vallejos.
Cover and Interior Layout: Nick Zelinger, www.NZGraphics.com

Library of Congress Cataloging-in-Publication Data
ISBN: 978-0-9903739-1-9 (soft cover)

First Edition

Printed in the USA

Contents

Introduction

I didn't expect to write two novels on the *cuadernos* that arrived at my home in the early fall of 2011. I just felt like the Lord was standing behind me and tapped me on the shoulder and said, "You, take this story, you have the strength and the history to share my Word". What I learned was fascinating, the deep understanding of the spiritual world, where it originated, why it originated and now its purpose.

The first book was *Portal of Light*, an anthropological non-fiction history of the Judaic cryptic community from southern Colorado and northern New Mexico. It's an in-depth and vast story that links to history and challenges of a hidden community, a family calling for their *Mashiach* — Messiah. I knew then the real story disclosed by the Portal was the original hand of Creation of our world or the work of the Higher Being God.

This companion second book, *Shared Lives, Twin Sun* brings the *cuadernos* to the now, the today. Just as societies change and people forget who they are and where they are from, a story is told to remind society that the Lord provided this Earth that we so graciously live upon. A changing society has its limits and to challenge the laws of Creation, carries a steep price to be paid. A reminder of who created this Earth, by the cryptic Ladino group that would preserve the Word of the Lord.

"The best fiction is the best fact," wrote American William Faulkner. This is how I felt when I wrote this novel. The characters the Chairwomen, Conjunto and the Father are real assemblages of people that I have spent time with and I've gleaned much from their life experiences. What is also real is the Ladino's community request for the arrival of the Messiah to arrive.

The chapter titled *"The Great Veal of Concealment"* is pure gold, a fact-based sharing of the Judaic concealment at home, in prayer and in the *Morada*. Just as the knowledge of the cosmos is shared slowly, so is this sharing of the concealment of a concealed community. Lastly, the divulgence of the origin of the Portal of Light and its purpose is a concept for all family members to remember.

I write this in loving memory of my parents, EAG and JRG, and other parents that traveled north for work and liberty in their sacrifice for their families. *Cariño por mis hijos*, EBG, ASG, ABG, ESG.

Anthony Garcia

Foreword

The Portal of Light

The Portal of Light originates from the *Semano*, a term for heaven located in the Capricorn Constellation in the southern hemisphere of our galaxy. In the play *"Jornado de Exódo,"* clues were provided to establish the location of the First Sun-*Semano* in the Capricorn. This star a blue — white — burned out star called Dabih Major, was 8 billion years old and four times as big as our current sun. Known as a planetary nebula or white dwarf star, later gave life to the planets in our Milky Way. The Hubble Space Telescope located Dabih Major in 2003, and it's known as galaxy cluster MS2137.3-2353.

Judaic mystics and later Kaballah theorists that benefited from the mystics' insights, placed clues in the *"Jornado de Exódo"* play that establish the velocity of the Portal and the relative distance of Earth to the home of the Portal's origination. Then, with the modern knowledge of the functioning of both Dark Matter and Dark Energy, the capability of a Portal to exist has been substantiated.

The Sumerian and Native American Hopi cosmology also knew where the star was located. That was shared with only those with knowledge of the cosmos in each community. It was preserved as concealed body of wisdom available only to a select few.

The most recent interpreters of this wisdom share this by use of the term *Duende* — a mysterious force that everyone senses but no philosopher can explain. An earth spirit that assists artists to rise to evocation in their art performance far beyond their natural ability can be visualized, but not quantified.

The story of the Portal of Light travels a long journey, arriving at the special land and ambiance of the 33° parallel in the new world, the same latitude as Jerusalem the Holy. This story of the *Jornado de Exódo* preserved for a future time to be shared at a time of duress and necessity. That time is now.

"To view the cosmos in a logical form is the natural weakness of Science, the effort to quantify the invisible — the surreal — the faith, is the real art form of the cosmos."

Anthony Garcia

CHAPTER 1

The Passage

Washington Park and the Delivery Man
Denver, Colorado 2011

Washington Park in Denver, Colorado, was a one-day ride from Northern New Mexico in the early fall of 2011. Conjunto was asked to deliver these two *cuadernos* — notebooks to a stranger, only known to him as Antonio. He was to have the knowledge to understand these writings and be able to translate them from Spanish to English. These *cuadernos* contain an archaic Spanish, which very few speak any more. *How can a man so far away from New Mexico in this age possess this knowledge?* Conjunto wondered. *But I am just the delivery man.*

Having arrived in Denver, Conjunto veered off I-25 at the Downing exit in his sky-blue, two-door 1966 Impala with a slanted back window that only the coolest of the cool drove. He felt like the main *chingon*, the main man in his ride.

He made an immediate right turn into Washington Park, "*A la ma*" he said to himself, "what are all of these pretty, yellow-haired girls running around the park doing? They almost do not have clothes on. I see why this guy lives here. He got what you call 'pinash.'"

He then made a right on Lafayette and saw Antonio's house. His Native American instincts arose as he noticed a significance event at the entry of the home. He then parked in front of the house. The red brick entry way was an oval archway portal, which called to mind a line in the play from the *cuaderno*, *The Portal of Light*. The tan stucco exterior and deep red accents around the house reminded him of the homes in Santa Fe, New Mexico.

As Conjunto got out of his car, he was decked out in his high-top, black dress boots with Cuban heals, his slim jean legs snuggled neatly over the boots that had silver metal taps on the front and back of the soles. His shirt was a simple, white short sleeve with a collar. A package of Lucky Strikes could be rolled up on his sleeve. His brown skin held no wrinkles, and with his collar-length, jet-black hair, he gave the impression that he was someone who gave gray hairs rather than got gray hairs.

Conjunto was not his real name; he was named this for the mixed ensemble of his background. He was a primary mix of Spanish and Native American from the tribe of Acoma cliff dwellers. What he was especially known for was his Christian faith, yet by all outward standards, he would appear as a *cholo* — a street guy with an attitude. "Hey *ese, que pasó*"?

He smoothly strutted up to the door with that ever-cool sound of metal taps, chin-chin, chin-chin, when he noticed something suspicious, a caution that told his street wise senses that he had arrived at the correct home. Stepping into the interior portal of the entry way, he noticed markings of blood slashed within the doorway. He recalled a lesson from his medicine-man grandfather that these are the signs of the *Sephardim* — *Seraditas*, the hidden Judaic community from old Spain.

Suddenly a young-looking man opened the portal door. "You are from New Mexico." As Antonio glanced around the tall man in the doorway, he spotted the classic car shining in the shade on the street. "I really dig your car. My brother had one like that. That is some style! The needle on the speedometer crosses practically across the entire dashboard from 0 to 120 mph," he said, pondering whether to let this outlander into his home, as he was expecting someone much older.

However, when he noticed the black leather bag in his visitor's right hand, Antonio said, "*Entra*" and stepped to the side to let this strange puzzle piece into his home.

"I can dig it," said Conjunto as he swaggered into the home with his shoulders swaying slightly side to side.

Conjunto was now spellbound by his surroundings as he looked around the *sala* — living room. He first noticed an antique gun cabinet, a tube radio cabinet from the 1940s, and a fireplace that possessed an arch portal opening. The second room entry was an even larger portal where he noticed the *Famila Cosmico* — Cosmic Family painting, set in the San Luis Valley of Colorado. More importantly, he recognized a handmade bench from the *Hermano Penitentes*, ordinarily kept within their *Morada*, the small chapels of the *Hermanos Penitentes*, an item reserved only for those with insight from the "light."

"Let us move into the second room by the table," Antonio recommended.

Conjunto opened the black leather bag and removed the two *cuadernos* and placed them upon the dining room table. "I brought this to you on behalf of the Ladino-Judaic families. Do you think you can translate the writing of the ancient sacred writers?"

"I think I can," Antonio answered.

"I was told you help build satellites that go up in space and take pictures. How do you do that?" Conjunto asked, his tone of voice transforming from the Cholo dialect to a matter-of-fact English dialect.

"I am able to configure the satellite," Antonio answered. "You are an *Hermano Penitente* from one of the tribes. You understand the Spirituality of Christ?" Antonio hurriedly asked.

"Yes, I was told this is very important to the faithful of our community. No one has been able to break this code. The year 2012 is approaching, and this must be broken soon. Can you do this? We need to know."

"I believe I can," Antonio said directly to the stranger.

Conjunto looked intently at Antonio. He knew the importance of this translation. He then turned around and walked briskly out the front door.

Antonio held the two leather *cuadernos* in his hand, thinking to himself, *This is perplexing; they are so different from one another.* As he opened the pages of the first *Alabado cuaderno,* he noticed that there were listed songs of praise, yet what was unique was that a number of Ladino words were used throughout the text. The lyrics were beautifully scribed, yet something mysterious surrounded this specific *cuaderno.* He would later realize that *la Marca* — the Mark of the Covenant — was indelibly hidden within one of the *Alabados.*

The second anonymous *cuaderno* was four times as thick, but not one *Alabado* song appeared. Upon looking closely, he could see that it was structured as a play, yet written in an *Alabado* style and feel. Antonio knew that the *Hermandad* — the Brotherhood — did not perform theatre plays, as this form of sharing its faith was not their custom or style of educating their members.

As Antonio began to read the play, he realized that he could interpret the Ladino words if he listened through his mother's voice because he had heard his mother using the same vocabulary, word structure and cadence. This story certainly came through her family, he thought to himself initially. Antonio's mother's father and her brothers were *Hermanos,* and all helped build the *Morada* in their hometown in New Mexico.

As Antonio read through the play, he realized that the play shares an alternate story of the birth Jesus of Nazareth. He wondered, *Could this be possible? Could the Bible story of the Magi following a star to meet the baby Jesus not be correct?* In this play, it's a group of shepherds who follow a Portal of Light to encounter the Emmanuel.

It is this initial mystery that infused a curiosity into Antonio that did not let him rest or sleep. The play arrived untitled and written anonymously. *This story is scribed or passed down, but where and who are the writers of this story?*

Antonio realized that the use of 16th Century Castilian Spanish was a major part of this play and that he would need assistance to translate it. He contacted a Harvard-educated professor at Regis University, whose specialty was 16th century Spanish poetry. He wondered if she would recognize the Ladino or Hebrew words or if the characters would tip her off that the work had a Judaic tradition. Having realized the delicacy of the work and the rare history of this story, Antonio immediately became a defender of the play. After working with her for three months on the translation, it became clear that she did not recognize any Ladino or Hebrew words, nor did she see it as a Judaic work. *Just as the original writers intended*, Antonio thought to himself.

As if written in his DNA code, Antonio became a guard of the manuscript, for he knew organically that it was his responsibility to conceal the original writers and the identity of those who forwarded the play to him. Yet he did not expect that the sleuth that he had become would be enlightened to recognize the history of a story and community that had waited four centuries to be disclosed. What he would uncover would forever change his knowledge of how he viewed the cosmos and his own spirituality.

La Tribuna — The Bench

It was early in 2011 that Antonio brought *La Tribunal* — the Bench — into his home. He had obtained it from an inactive *Morada* — small chapel in Northern New Mexico to ensure that its spiritual power would forever be valued. Its presence signified the strength or backbone to carry the physical weight of a genuflecting body in the act of contrition that released bad deeds, and then where solemn pleas were disclosed. Antonio bore witness to these pleas and knew that the modern world, the politically correct world, would challenge the origin of Creation that was shared upon *La Tribunal*.

Within Antonio's home, the Bench provided a safe haven for the essence of judgment to be concealed for the Higher Being God. The solitary knowledge that the *Ladino Hermanos'* use of this splintered object to encapsulate one's spiritual relationship to the *Todo Poderoso* — the All Powerful One — had become the sole proprietorship of

Antonio and the Ladino families who had shared this awareness with him.

The plain rough-cut pinewood bench seemed innocent enough as it sat in a lonely corner of Antonio's *sala* — dining room — and showed no sign of importance to most onlookers. Yet to the *Ladino Hermanos*, this was a valued part of their customs, as the tribunal bench was the court of God used in the *Moradas* in New Mexico and Southern Colorado. Here, the *Ladino Hermanos* would kneel before the bench to share the errors of their lives and ask for forgiveness. Often, Ladinos asked the question why this community was chosen to bear the cryptic life they endured. Why must they live such a complicated, twin life — outwardly as a Catholic while inwardly as a Jew? When would the Messiah finally arrive to alleviate their pain?

La Tribunal was a place where, upon kneeling before it, one could bring the physical and spiritual burdens they bore as they leaned upon it in bowed reverence to the Lord. Acknowledging the presence of a Higher Being, one released his soul and consciousness to be judged, by a tribunal of judges, but here one would be scrutinized by the highest consciousness of the Almighty and All-knowing God. They sensed that the evaluation of one's intellect was the collective formation of a wide band of perception from a higher consciousness that worked collectively in its analysis of all matters. For them, judgment and counsel were not derived from a single contemplative process, as they did from a human mind.

Formed from simple, rough-cut, ¾- inch pinewood, the Bench was not more than three feet wide, with wide cut legs. Hand-saw marks provided a coarse feel and grooved texture of the forests from the mountain terrain that surrounds most *Moradas*.

The *Ladino Hermanos* knelt before the unfinished rough lumber, their concentration and meditation of prayer connected to the Higher Being, God, the wooded facia absorbing *sudor* — sweat — and *lagrimas* — tears as they dripped from their consoled faces of prayer and contrition made to the Lord.

Here, upon the bench, was borne, either internally or verbally, a venting of grief and the strain from the cryptic Judaic life as lived within a Christian society in the New World. Their anxiety and pressures were lifted to God himself, and these pleas were heard by the Lord. The common avowal, "*Why, Lord, have you placed us in such misery? It is your will for us to live this twin life, but for what purpose we do not understand.*" For some families, this twin life and repression began in 1598, and among these first arrivals — *los originales* —many felt that begging for their Judaic Messiah to deliver them was an absolute right.

Ladino Hermanos felt they had been placed in a Christian environment by the will of God to validate their faith, and they believed the Tribunal revealed why they were placed in the life they led. Their placement in a repressed environment, living twin lives, gave them an absolute right to request the coming of the Messiah, for this was their inheritance of living as a repressed Jew. This was an important factor for a future time when only a Messiah would be able to provide the remedy for a life distorted by humans themselves. Many non-Ladinos cannot understand the responsibility of living a twin-faith life while silently accepting their fate. Notwithstanding, most non-Ladino Christian and Judaic people do not grasp the fact that silence was their survival.

To the Ladino families, their duality of faith was a unique blend of spiritual responsibilities, for it still summoned them to uphold the Law of Moses while honoring the Emmanuel, whom they also accepted as the promised Messiah of old. The lifestyle of being both Jewish and Christian encumbered the *Ladino Hermanos* with a unique hardship, an atonement to sustain one's faith. The penance or payment of living this twin lifestyle was the burden of carrying the duality of faith while leading a concealed life and preserving their history within a Christian society.

Grateful and respectful of the life provided, Ladinos also regarded the Tribunal as a symbol of how the Lord bore the weight of their lives and carried them in time of need. Because life in New Spain was challenging and often dangerous for all, the Tribunal provided a comforting outlet for cleansing one's soul and instilling gratitude for survival in these harsh lands.

The depth of their prayer and divulgence of soul brought forward the ability to extract from within one's consciousness the secrets of the Kabbalah so as to understand how faith is related to the cosmos and how the Higher Being functions within Dark Matter and Dark Energy. Members of the Sefardim-*Seradita* community felt it was as if God was aware of their hardships and commitment to their faith, and for this, the faithful were bestowed with a deeper understanding of the Cosmos.

In the year 2012, the *cuadernos* brought Antonio the insight into the lengthy journey to disclose the origin of Creation. The *cuadernos* provided the wisdom to Antonio to disclose this knowledge from the Ladino families in the age of Aquarius. He learned that the *Ladino Hermanos* requested liberty from repression just as their Judaic precursors requested freedom from the Romans, emperors, and sackers. The Lord God had heard their ancestors' cries, and then appeared Jesus of Nazareth. The symbol for the carnation is to reincarnate, to seek the higher union of flesh of mankind with the higher being of God himself.

Hermitaño and Carnation
Sinai Mountains
High in current-day Libya
1 B.C.

For generations the Judaic mountain sheepherders had lived in the rugged and rocky Sinai Mountains, where they passed down their family skills of caring for sheep in tundra that provided sparse greenery. The high-altitude rock and dirt formation did not permit flowers or depth of plant life to grow in this dry land ambiance. Yet the Judaic sheepherders persisted, supported by their faith and their continued belief that one day the *Mashiach* — Messiah would *take the barren land and make it abundant and fruitful.* (*Ezekiel 36:29-30*)

These semi-nomadic sheepherders cared for their sheep, both day and night, constantly searching for quality grazing areas and water for their flocks. Close to dusk, each sheepherder rounded up a portion of the sheep in one area, placing oblong rocks in a circle around the gathering. This acted as an invisible fence that the sheep understood not to pass beyond. Dry branches, logs and sticks were gathered in the middle to be set aflame upon the appearance of the stars. Darkness provided a breathtaking view of the smoky Milky Way. The sheepherders sat around their campfire in reverence of the beauty of the stars, which words could not describe. It was here that the waiting and sharing of the *Mashiach* would be experienced. It was here that the a cappella prayer songs originated from the mystic shepherds and later became the *Alabados* style of writings among Ladinos.

The Sinai mountains separated the Great Sea of Sand, *Rúbal Al Khalid* to one side and the Mediterranean Sea to the other. These mountain ridges and valleys, known as *wadi*, run parallel to each other and ascend downward to their Judaic homelands in Israel.

The Bedouins wore long-sleeve shirts and loose fitting pants, typically of an earth color of tan or a faded blue. Dressed in their ancient Sudra headwear, made of white cotton and fashioned as a square scarf, they wrapped it once around the head and then fit it loosely to cover neck and back to prevent sunburn and dust blow. A sheepherder used a 5-6 foot- long staff as a guide to control the flock after first selecting one of the male rams to be the leader. A sling shot made of leather also was carried to hurl rocks at a runaway sheep to prevent it from leaving the herd.

The Bedouins appreciated the beauty of this terrain. Their life was rugged and simple but not without purpose. Living alone, far from Judea, they were without fear because of their faith and the knowledge of the Cosmos. They were known to some as Judaic Mystics and to others as Kabbalists. Connected deeply to the land, they possessed knowledge that the beginning of the age of Pisces would provide a very special event for the cosmos to behold. They knew the arrival of the *Mashiach* — Messiah was forthcoming.

Over 2000 years ago in the age of Pisces, two of these devout Judaic Bedouins, Jila and Tubal, were about to become caught up in the eternal plan of the Most High. The woman, Jila, was the leader of the shepherd group, who managed its flock high in the Sinai Mountains. Tubal was also an important sheepherder who was waiting for a special person to arrive and fulfill the prophecies from their sacred texts. On the appointed day, the shepherd Tubal was collecting a small group of sheep that had separated from the main group when he came across something that left him in total bewilderment. He found fields and fields of pink carnations in the barren and arid mountain rock of the Sinai. The vibrant, five-blossom flower had a fringed or scalloped edge. All shepherds at this time knew that carnations were a sign of new life or opportunity.

Tubal collected his sheep, ran back to the base camp and yelled out. "Jila, Jila, you must see this! It is a sign! Come, Come follow me!

Jila was preparing a *migas*, a late morning meal of wild spinach — *quelites*, onion and day-old bread. She stopped everything and followed Tubal to the field of carnations. "What is this?" she asked.

"These carnations are a sign, a sign of an incarnation that is to come. The pink carnation is a sign of reincarnation, perhaps the appearance of the coming of the Messiah. To reincarnate is to seek the higher union of flesh with the higher being God himself," explained Tubal. He will "take the barren land and make it abundant and fruitful."

"Each flower has five blossoms," Jila said. "I have never seen such beauty." Then Jila noticed an old man caring for these beautiful five-point flowers and called to him, "Old man, why are you caring for these flowers high in the mountains?"

The old man was an Hermitaño, a time traveler, who traveled alongside the Portal of Light into this galaxy on a mission for the Higher Being God. He had arrived on Earth before as witness to past experiences of the Judaic community and, therefore, was a witness to both positive and negative historic events. On this mission, his purpose was to disclose to the shepherds that a light was to appear overhead and that they join him and follow the Light, so they might also be witnesses to the birth of Emmanuel, the Messiah.

The old man was bent at his waist and held a blossom to smell. "This floral, spicy scent represents the giving love of a mother," he said. "There is no other way to describe this love. You feel it and know it, yet it can only be duplicated by the one to arrive."

"Who is to arrive?" Jila asked.

"An angel told me in my ear of the baby Messiah that is to be born," the stranger said.

Upon the Hermitaño's entrance into the Earth's atmosphere, he had adopted the sackcloth of a human skin and now dressed with one piece of men's clothing cinched at the midriff with a sash belt.

"May we invite you to speak with us?" Jila asked. "We are old shepherds and have never seen such beauty. Please come to our camp, as I was preparing a meal for our brethren."

The stranger joined the shepherds as they walked to the campsite. Never had the shepherds seen such a being before in these highlands, and were curious about this caretaker of the field of carnations. *Did he plant these flowers of vibrant color in this rocky soil?* they asked themselves. *Where did he garner the fresh water that such beauty can derive from in these parts?*

Hermitaño was aware that this group of shepherds was on the cusp of witnessing a rare event that would stop time; he had come there to participate and feel what this experience was like. Afterward, he would report this emotion and how this event changed mankind to the Higher Being God.

"Tell us sir, how did you come across to care for these plants of artistry? Tubal asked.

"An angel foretold to me of the coming of the Messiah, and the carnations are the sign of his arrival," the stranger explained.

Both Tubal and Jila looked at each other. "Tell us, what is your name?" Jila asked.

"I am the Hermitaño."

"What is to come?" Tubal asked.

"A Portal of Light will soon cross above the field of carnations. This must be followed to Bethlehem where the Messiah will arrive," Hermitaño explained, for these shepherders were to be witnesses to the Emmanuel's birth.

"What does this Portal look like?" Jila asked.

"I do not know. I only know the time is now. The Judaic people have waited long for this sign. The land will be *abundant and fruitful.* The carnations — these are certainly a sign. Whenever have you seen such beauty in these unforgiving mountains?" the Hermitaño asked.

"We have never seen such a site. Tell us, where does the Portal come from?" Jila asked.

"The Portal derives from heaven, the *Semano.*" The Hermitaño explained slowly that the name for heaven was labeled by the Judaic mystics and that the journey they were about to take would bring forward the Emmanuel, sent by the Higher God himself.

The Hermitaño's Journey
Sinai Mountains
Camp of *Shepherd Hermanos*
1 B. C.

The more Tubal and Jila listened to the hermitaño, the more curious they were to understand where this strange being came from. "Tell us more about where you're from and how you got here," Jila urged.

"The journey from Capricornus is exhilarating," their visitor replied, enthusiastically. "I traveled as a subconscious fragment on the Portal of Light, able to visualize and recognize all landmarks that I passed. Capricornus is located in the southern sector of this universe of vast space and emptiness. Entities, such as myself, travel at such speed that time actually slows down. This effect is known to time travelers as Spatial Time in Dark Matter. Tangible objects, such as asteroids, gas, rays, and rocks, we approach and pass by, for we travel on a plane of matter that does not interact, yet we are able to view such objects."

"How long was the journey?" Tubal asked.

"I left two years prior to your time to arrive on your planet from the Capricornus-Sun star, a long-ago, burned-out, white quasar star. Although billions of years in age, an inward mushroom appearance is still warm from its billions of eons of smoldering."

Still curious about their guest, Jila pressed him further. "What exactly is an hermitaño?"

"The Hermitaño is a time traveler, landing in a time frame to interact with human beings as they experience significant time events in Judaic history. It is an entity that transforms into a human being to witness and experience the life here for a brief moment in time and then report back to the Higher Being God. The human beings we encounter, such as yourselves, reside in a historic event in time and share the life experience with the time traveler."

Tubal then asked, "What lies within the Dark Matter you mentioned?"

"This is where the invisible becomes visible, behind the dark curtain, the most fascinating part of the cosmos. The Dimensions hold ageless and boundless beauty of cosmic entities that lived within their own confines. While invisible to the human's naked eye, they are thriving and exploding with life behind this Dark Matter Curtain.

The Dimensions live separate unto themselves and respect the lives of beings from other Dimensions."

Fascinated, Tubal pressed him further. "Does each Dimension have its own purpose or meaning for existing?"

"Yes, a series of mature civilizations do exist that have mastered the knowledge of Dark Matter. You will not see explosions of energy, the furious eye of the Dark Holes or the uncontrolled star explosions. Rather, a calm management of the force of Dark Matter is used for each dimension's own purpose. From an outward appearance, a large dimension does not mean they possess more control of dark matter than a smaller dimension. On the contrary, they actually have less control."

"When you entered our Milky Way system, what did you think of its beauty?" Jila wondered with excitement.

Quite stunning. I entered from what you would call your Southern Hemisphere. The planets were in alignment — to the East, the dry-fire planets of Venus, Saturn, and Pluto; to the West, the wet planets of Mars and Jupiter. I passed the water moons of Jupiter, then the asteroid belt surrounding the galaxy. I caught sight of Mars, where the shallow mountains and valleys that once held water were remarkable. We passed by your Sun, ever exploding with fire balls and massive electrodes, yet one could hear the inner hum of its generating force. Finally, I arrived midway through the human calendar month of January in a time frame in the rural mountainous regions of the Sinai to join with you, Hermano Shepherds. I am here to lead you through the Portal of Light to Bethlehem to greet the Messiah, for we will be witnesses to His birth."

"How are you and the Portal able to travel such long distances?" Tubal asked.

"It is called the Plank Propeller technology. We are able to use this technology to travel at compressed light years of velocity. Yet, first, one must gain access to the Dark Matter via the Cosmic

Adapter, an advanced mechanism that will connect your earthly world to the dimensional world," Hermitaño explained.

"Will there be future times when the Judaic community must conceal themselves to survive?" Tubal asked.

"Yes, there will be a writing that concealed the Judaic history for almost a quarter of a century. It possessed a purpose," The Hermitaño explained.

The Writing of the *Jornado de Exódo* play
in the *Cuaderno* — Notebook
The Year 1733
Near Santa Cruz de la Cañada
New Mexico Territory

In the year 1733 near the small town of *Santa Cruz de la Cañada* in what is presently northern New Mexico, Pedro was about to begin the writing of a cryptic play that would conceal the history of the Ladino community in a Christian recruitment play. Pedro descended from one of the Ladino families that first migrated into this area when it was still under the rule of New Spain. Their ability to conceal their Judaic history was indeed a rare ability, for it held many special attributes that enabled the preservation of their faith.

The majestic beauty of the mountains gave way to the semi-arid landscape of willow, pine, scrub bushes, and a small creek and, at night, an expansive view of the Milky Way constellation. The sweet smell of piñon wood filled the air from small mud-built *casitas* — little houses scattered throughout the valley and blending with the scenery.

Pedro had just lit the *lenya* — firewood in the fireplace just before sundown when he saw a man standing outside his adobe. He walked over to the front window, opened the shutters further, and looked outside. The man looked vaguely familiar, but Pedro was not certain who he was. He was dressed in work pants, boots, and a white undershirt under a flannel, long-sleeve blue shirt. His coat was made of leather, worn just as all workers wear their outer garments, loose and unzipped, yet ready for the next job.

Pedro opened his front door and yelled, "*Porqué estás en mi tierra?* — Why are you on my land?"

The stranger answered, "I am here looking for Pedro. I am an old friend of your grandfather. He asked that I talk to you."

Pedro's grandfather had died over 15 years prior. He had beeen one of the pioneers in this land and had maintained many of the customs and languages that were native to this new territory.

"May I come in and talk with you? I know your grandfather would appreciate that I took the time to locate and speak with you," the stranger said.

Pedro recognized the dialect of this stranger, for he used the colonial Spanish mixed with Ladino words and a style that reminded him of his grandfather. This dialect originated solely from one local, a native-born Ladino.

"Tell me, who are you?" Pedro asked.

"I am known as the Hermitaño, known as a traveler of sorts. I used to live in this territory. I made the voyage from old Spain, spoke all of the needed languages and dialects and, lastly, knew your grandfather well," the Hermitaño said. "Do you think I could enter your home and speak with you of the past?"

"*Entra* — come in," Pedro said. "*Sientanse* — please sit down. Would you like coffee, made fresh this morning?"

"*Un tasa de café, si* — A cup of coffee, yes." The stranger sat at the hand-made table and chairs, made of rough-cut pine and 3-inch steel nails. The original pioneers had made all of their furniture from their own land. Pedro brought out coffee cups and saucers and poured the fresh brew for the both of them. A comfort and calm was forged by these two rural men, dressed in similar fashion, who spoke the same dialect and maintained the same mannerisms.

Then, out of nowhere, the Hermitaño asked, "How do you plan to write this anonymous play?"

Stunned, Pedro looked even more intensely at this stranger. *How did he possibly know that I planned to write a cryptic play?* Pedro thought to himself.

"Your grandfather told me that he shared with you the knowledge of the Ladino community, and he thought that one day you would figure out a way to safely share this story," the Hermitaño explained.

A skeptical Pedro answered, "Tell me something that demonstrates you have this knowledge."

"There existed a First Sun in the sky, known only to a few communities." The Hermitaño disclosed in a lowered voice.

"The knowledge of the First Sun was only available to those with the profound knowledge of the "light," Pedro mused. Since he, himself, was one of the very few that was privy to this knowledge, he immediately relaxed, and his doubt for this stranger subsided. Surprisingly, he found himself opening his soul to this outsider, as he began to tell him about the historic account he was planning to conceal in a play, beginning with the title *The Jornado de Exódo* — The Journey of Exodus.

"There must be a way to preserve our Judaic heritage without the awareness of the Spanish Catholics!" Pedro said.

"In Judaic history, there have been many efforts to preserve their history, whether it be concealed or not. In the siege of Masada, the Jews battled the Romans to the very end. This history is never to be forgotton," Hermitaño answered.

"That is what I have been thinking. Let me share this with you. The Spanish friars have been recruiting Native American souls in all of this newly discovered territory. They are using various methods to share Christianity, such as songs, music, poems and theatre. A recently written play, titled *Los Pastores*, is being used to indoctrinate the native people. My thought is to write a version of this play, concealing historical clues and figures within the writings that only a person of both Ladino or Hebrew background would be able to recognize," Pedro explained.

Hermitaño recognized what Pedro was trying to accomplish. "You must have a deep understanding of Judaic history, languages, geography and a strong grasp of the writings of both the Bible and the Torah to be able to do what you desire. Your writings must be profound, yet specific, to pull this off."

"They are," Pedro answered. "Our families originate from Rabbinic backgrounds. We are educated in various histories and speak Ladino, Spanish, Tewa and, to a degree, Hebrew and Aramaic. We have historically written the very profound *Alabados*, the songs of the Spanish psalms. Some of us have written prayers, Christian songs, church doctrine and plays in the past and continue to do so today."

The Hermitaño queried him, "Tell me this. Has the Judaic community written Christian works before?"

"Yes. The Passion Play — *Los Pastores*, was written just last year by Miguel de Quintana of Santa Cruz de la Cañada. I am going to use some characters and concepts from that play and intermix other characters to create a Jewish Remnant to be shared among the Ladino families."

Quintana's creative works influenced the entire community and was seen as a threat to the church Friars' affairs, as they reported to the Holy Office of the Inquisition that Quintana was a Judaic heretic. This began a five-year investigation of Quintana and culminated in an accord that would prevent Quintana from writing Christmas plays and limit the scope of his writing. During this process, the play *Jornado de Exódo* — Journey of Exodus was written anonymously

"I am also going to write this in an *Alabado* style, similar to the *Alabados* format used by the *Hermanos Penitentes*. I read them in the *cuadernos* they use when sharing prayers with their members," Pedro explained. "We will hide the play in a *cuaderno*, and it will

appear as a play written by a Christian Hermano. The stanza structure, sentence length and rhythm of the writing will be the same as
they appear in the *Alabados* psalm. The story in the play will at least,
on the surface, appear to be told from a Christian reference point.

"Let me get this right," the Hermitaño interjected. "You plan to
hide the Judaic camouflaged writing of a play in a Christian *Alabados*
format, using a *cuaderno*? You have got *cojones* — balls to do this.
"Where are you going to hide these *cuadernos*?"

"We will hide them with the Judaic *Hermanos* who are members
of the *Hermandad* — Brotherhood within the *Moradas*," Pedro
explained.

"That is extremely dangerous! They are very devout and practice
the Catholic faith of the Hermandad. And at the same time, you
want to hide a Judaic play in their midst?"

"The *Ladino Hermanos* and their families will conceal this work
and ration this play to Ladino newcomers in this territory as a reference to their Hebrew history and act as a Jewish Remnant of survival," Pedro said with excitement in his eyes.

"Where will you meet?" the Hermitaño asked.

"We can meet secretly in the *Moradas*."

"But the *Moradas* are the small chapels where the Catholic
Hermandad perform their services and practices, right?" the Hermitaño asked.

"Right," Pedro confirmed.

"You are risking the lives of every member of the Judaic community by making this move. Do you understand that it only takes one
person to talk or one person to discover the play and decipher its
contents? Remember what happened to Quintana."

"Yes, but if we don't, we will be known as the Dead Law of Moses.
Every community has its price to pay, and this risk is for survival,"
Pedro said decisively.

"This is extremely bold and I realize that your community must
go to lengths to survive, yet you are hiding in plain sight. Will every

Morada have this play?" the Hermitaño queried, still unsure of the plan.

"Possibly," Pedro said.

Hermitaño pondered. "Then a small Judaic community could exist across this territory."

"That is my hope," Pedro answered with a firm voice.

"I will use clues from diverse cultures and references to Jewish places and history, clearly a coded message to preserve the Judaic history. The use of words and characters from Ladino, Hebrew, Arabic, Greek and Italian origin will be shared in the play. Even the most educated will think these words are spelled incorrectly or will not understand their origin," Pedro explained.

"I will use the characters of Jila, Bacto and Tevano to underscore the origins of these players from the Greek Tragedies, *The Iliad* and *The Odyssey*, by Homer," Pedro continued. "These provide the broad application of the balance of power of good vs. evil, of the yin and yang, as a preserved Greek tragedy story telling method," Pedro explained. "This will show that the original writers are educated and literate in arts as well."

Pedro proceeded to share who the major characters in his play would be:

Jila is the female slave in the Greek Tragedy *The Iliad*, by Homer, written in 1250 B.C. She was an important character in the play, for she is one of two characters to confront *El Diablo* and is the leader of the Hermano-Shepherds group as it descends the Sinai mountains.

Bacto or Bacchus in Homer's book T*he Odyssey* illustrates the depth of historical knowledge of a Greek tragedy and mythology.

Tevano, translated from Greek to Spanish, means Greek. This was the third Greek character that shined and demonstrated the influence of the writing style and mode of expression that the Greek style of the balance of power had upon the writers of *Jornado de Exódo.*

The *Jornado de Exódo* play was modeled after the ancient Greek thought and literature, where there lay a balance of two principles: the feminine vs. the masculine, the balance between good and evil. *El Diablo* represents the feminine, pleasure-pain darkness character that aligns with Pluton-Hades the King of the Underworld, Lucifer, and Herod in the play. The masculine Archangel Michael is the Sun-God, the light dream, beauty, clarity, self-control and aligns with the Emmanuel, Joseph and Mother Mary.

"The *Jornado de Exódo* play created a great tragedy of epic design, control over the in-depth knowledge of mind and soul of mankind versus control and fate of the Emmanuel's future. In this play, the drama will counterbalance the battle between *El Diablo* versus Michael Arc Angel and the Emmanuel," Pedro explained.

"How will the Ladino families know that these characters are from a Greek tragedy?"Hermitaño asked.

"Our families are home-taught, so they were aware of the writings of Homer, both the New and Old Testaments and the Judaic history lineage. We smuggled books from Old Spain, including the Torah, the Kabbalah and Zohar writers Moshe Cordoviero and Moshe de Leon, the Ladino dictionary and, lastly, the Book of Ferrer, the Ladino Bible. These are all part of our history," Pedro explained.

"What you are saying is that the most knowledgeable readers will look further into the scripture and realize that Jila originates from elsewhere?" Hermitaño asked.

"Yes, that is how it is hidden. Part of this is to make the visible invisible. The Jila character, in actuality, comes from the Book of Daniel, but I want the direction of non-Ladino readers to think that her character originates from the Greek tradition, as do Bacto and Tevano," Pedro said.

"You Sephardim are very insightful in the art of cryptology. Moshe Codoviero and his students taught you well," The Hermitaño observed. "Their life philosophy of concealment was survival. Would you be using specific historical figures such as Abraham or Noah an important Judaic person in the story?"

"No, those smart friars and priests would recognize them!" Pedro said. "We can use the words *Dio* for Dios — God, *dise* for dice — says, *alegre* for *allegre* — happy, and *lovo* for *lobo* — wolf, and *firmament* for firmament, as these words will be recognized as Castilian Spanish, and they are pronounced the same as well. Words such as *redema* for redeem, *abora* for the dawning, *padesco* for suffering and *parro* for to be born will also be used."

The Hermitaño interpreted, "These are all Ladino words. Are you also able to use Hebrew words?"

"Yes, *Tafila* — prayer, *Durme* — sleep, *Mortificar* — damage, *Asmodeo* — *Asmodeus* the King Demon from the Kabbalah, and Tubal, grandson of Noah" Pedro said.

The character Tubal is the direct link to Judaic heritage, son of Japeth, grandson to Noah from the Genesis story of the flood and the building of Noah's Ark. After the flood, Tubal founded European cities like the port city of Tarragona in Spain. He represented the ancestor relationship of Judea to the Iberian peninsula of both Spain and Portugal.

"You have taken great risk with these Hebrew words and names. Are you certain that this play will be shared with only the Ladino families?" Hermitaño said sharply.

"The Ladino community has been very loyal to one another as well as secretive. Remember, secrecy is survival," Pedro explained further. "I used some words that are a specific reference to Judaic history like, 'Lepio Santo.' While many thought this referred to a holy saint, this actually referred to the character Lepio, translated from Italian, which means temple. I used the word *Travado* — Exodus and the Hebrew word *Tafila* — for prayer."

The Italian word *Lepido* translates from the word *Temple* and the *Holy Temple of Jerusalem*, plundered by the King Shishak of Egypt in 925 B.C. *Travado* — to extract or remove people designates the times when the Judaic community has been forced to emigrate to another country, the same as in their exodus from Egypt after the plundering. The Hebrew word *Mortificar* means to damage or mortify. "This links specifically to Judaic history of Exodus, the pain of sacking our Temple and the damage inflicted."

"Never to be forgotten," Hermitaño added.

"We use the word *Rubal* in the story, referring to the Rubál al Khalid desert, the largest sea of sand in current-day Saudi Arabia," Pedro said.

"What does sand have to do with this story?" Hermitaño looked puzzled.

"Nothing. This is a word that likely most readers will never figure out. The word refers to the sea sand desert that laid on the other side of the Sinai mountains. This is where the *Hermanos* and their flock of sheep begin their arduous journey in the Lebanese mountains traversing downward toward Bethlehem to the cave to meet the Emmanuel," Pedro explained.

"We placed sentences written by first century historian and Judaic General Flavius Josephus in the story. He is a role model for the Sephardim community, you know," Pedro said.

"As you know, he was viewed as a traitor to the Judaic community," Hermitaño said to show Pedro he also had knowledge of Judaic history. Then his curiosity finally surfaced with the crucial question: "Who is the Emmanuel to you?"

"To me, Emmanuel is a sign that God is with us and this was the most important message," Pedro answered with conviction. "Yet to the Christian reader that comes across the term Emmanuel in this play, they will likely connected to the passages best explained in Mathew 1:23, *The virgin will conceive and give birth to a son, and they will call him Immanuel."*

"This is a riddle, a puzzle for those familiar with the great lineage of Judaic history; otherwise, it is hidden in plain sight. You are preserving the historical past of the Judaic time line," The Hermitaño observed.

"Your community possesses an ability to hide in plain sight. Where was this skill obtained?" Hermitano asked.

"Concealment is the application of Moshe Cordoviero's PARDES to conceal your presence in any life situation by means of words, phrase, philosophies and camouflage in any form necessary. For the Ladino community, to hide was to endure hardships. This was how this story is accepted as genuine, for they understood the sacrifice it took to survive."

Hermitaño still sounded skeptical."You think you can hide an entire play without detection? You have got some *cojones* — balls! You are taking a great risk that this story will remain within Ladino families. What are the chances of this working?"

Pedro pondered and looked up to the sky. "There is no limit to the ability of survival, he said. It is the remnant of faith has that kept this community living, and that is why this has worked."

"When in the future will the play be shared?" Hermitaño queried.

"At the determination of a turning point in the future, when the values of the people of faith are no longer respected and are repressed. Then a message forward will be sent, and the story of this cryptic play will be released," Pedro announced prophetically.

CHAPTER 2

The Riddle of the
Cuadernos - Notebooks

Denver, Colorado
Early Fall 2011

The morning had started like any ordinary day. Antonio had made his chicken green chile with skinned tomatoes, garlic, and onion, all from his garden. His chile was made soupy by design and cooked on simmer. The sweet, pungent aroma of roasted green chile had filled his home, when a simple knock on his door and a stranger who entered provided him with a mystery that would occupy his existence for the rest of his life.

Antonio had taken a call earlier from Ladino families, whose names he could never reveal, and was told that a *cuaderno* would arrive that fall day from an important source. He had had previous contact with these families when he provided translations of both Castilian and Ladino Spanish *Alabados*. This call was different, though, as it was an urgent request to help them save something that was about to be lost. This time he was asked to translate and decipher the encrypted messages and share their revelations. This puzzled him, for at no time was he ever asked to do something this crucial.

When the messenger arrived, Antonio was expecting a mature person with experience, not a *cholo vato* — street guy at his doorstep. Back in the day, he and his friends described that unique kind of dude as a "cat," a person with his own singular personality. At first Antonio did not understand the enormity of the task, but when this cholo, who called himself Conjunto, said that the Ladino families wanted a translation by 2012, he was bewildered. *Why? What was so vital in this translation,* he asked himself. *A lengthy translation could take me three months by itself. I have a small business to run, my teenage kids are at South High School and the Denver Center for International Studies.*

Conjunto was aware of Antonio's background with the U.S. Department of Defense and that he had worked on a satellite. Conjunto knew Antonio was a person of knowledge and would protect the identities of the Ladino families. Yet he said they were unable to break the code by 2012. *What code? Was the code a number, a formula, a symbol, a matrix? What was he referencing?*

The two *cuadernos* created a puzzle that had not left Antonio's soul since they were laid next to each other upon the glass cover of his dining room table. The thick brown leather notebooks carried upon the fascia a symbol of the crescent leaves and spiral wire at its top to flip open its pages. The first *cuaderno* he opened was familiar to him, as it contained the numbered Spanish *Alabados* — songs of praise that would be translated into English.

The ability to translate both archaic and Ladino Spanish is special. It was passed on from the womb of the mother, for only she knew that a specific child can listen to and grasp this capability. This oral tradition is passed down from the soul. No school or book can train to hear the sound of your *antipasado* — history.

The second *cuaderno* puzzled Antonio. The notebook was four to five times as thick and contained a drama that was not in the *Alabados* song format, shared among the Hermandad and the *Hermanos* Penitentes. These are a confraternity or brotherhood sect of the Catholic religion that preserves the Passion week reenactment annually and is the oldest formal organization in the state of New Mexico. It is within this authority that the use of the songs of *Alabados* were used to preserve the Christian faith. As I opened the notebook, I realized these were not songs of praise, but rather they resembled the writing of a play, concealed in a *Alabados* format with five to eight words per line.

Written in a flowing, archaic Spanish, this story had been scribed and passed down over hundreds of years, yet written in a specific manner in order to preserve its authenticity. Yet Antonio knew from Conjunto there was a code. He wondered if the indigenous Kabbalah was part of this code he referred to, though few cultures preserve this awareness. Could it be possible that this work, which has few equals, was a rare story originated from Ladino families, that concealed its own unique story? *For what reason*, Antonio asked himself."

Antonio looked at the last page and found the date of November 1931, the last time it had been scribed.

The Portal of Light and the Cosmos

"Religion pretends to know something about science.
Faith is believing in something in the absence of evidence."
~ **Carl Sagan, astrophysicist**

In the home of Pedro with the Hermitaño
1733, New Mexico Territory

"The play we had written contains the technology of faith. Did you know this?" Hermitaño asked Pedro. "What we wrote describes how the Portal of Light revealed the dimensional capability of the Higher Being God."

"The Portal? The Portal holds the key to understanding the Spiritual Universe?" Pedro asked, his eyes wide with excitement.

"Yes. The story goes beyond the historical story of Judea and is secretly woven into both the numerical and conceptual clues to expose the mystery of the faith universe," Hermitaño said, seeing Pedro's disbelieving face.

Pedro lifted his head and looked off into a cloudless, blue sky. "I remember you placed a word in the play, what was it? *Carnacíon* — Carnation — more than once, as in a field of Carnations."

"Yes, high in the amber-colored Sinai mountains, on their barren, arid and rocky slopes, there appeared fields of pink carnations to the shepherds. These flowers with zigzagged petals arrived during the Judaic New Year in September, Rosh Hashana. It is very cold and snowy at that time of the year," The Hermitaño explained

"The Shepherd-*Hermanos* interpreted this as a sign of a forth-coming, the sign of the arrival of the Messiah, for whom they had been waiting for centuries," he Hermitaño explained.

"The shepherds finding fields of flowers created an alternate story of the birth of the Emmanuel, so the clue was the carnation," Pedro said realizing the answer.

"What does the pink carnation mean to you mystics, you Kabbal-ists?" Hermitaño asked.

"Pink is the color of love to us, and love is healing." Pedro answered but continued with a question for Hermitaño. "What is this Portal of Light you keep referring to?"

"The Portal of Light has a special role in human existence. It confirms the spiritual relationship between the Higher Being God, of a higher dimension and the lower dimension of mankind. The Portal is a conduit, a segue providing a message of enlightenment of such importance that it enters our atmosphere to illuminate the place of birth of a child whose philosophies and sacrifice will forever change the human values of life on Earth." Hermitaño looked straight into Pedro's eyes to see if he understood his explanation.

Still curious, Pedro continued his inquiry. "But how does the Portal of Light function?"

"The Portal travels through the invisible and non-reflective Dark Matter and Dark Energy of the universe. It is light years in length and can travel at light speed. It arrives with a purpose, to enlighten the path for the shepherds to follow to ensure Emmanuel will not be born on cold straw, no love or warmth in a cool cave."

Pedro asked, "Can you share with me what the Portal looks like in the cosmos?

Artist Robert Maestas' 2015 drawing of the Portal of Light

"The Portal arrived from a higher dimension and was fabricated to be able to travel vast distances to shed light on the birth of the Emmanuel," the Hermitaño said. The sound was reminiscent of sweeping leaves off a concrete path with a millet broom, yet following the rhythm of a 3/4 to 6/8 count of the flamenco guitar standard of the Guajira travel genre," the Hermitaño explained.

"The original Judaic mystics were musicians," Pedro added, "so they would have recognized what they heard. But how did it make these sounds? Is there sound in Cosmic Space?"

"The sound resembles the quiver of vibrating plank strands as the portal enters our atmosphere. The plank interchanges with our oxygen-H2O-rich atmosphere to create a unique chorus, performed as one, almost as a backdrop of notes to the energy field itself,"

Hermitaño explained, moving his hands in a circular fashion above his head.

"In writing the play, you used the phrase, '*dos en un vos*' — two in one voice. Does this deal with the portal?" Pedro asked.

"The *two-in-one voice* is part of the formula that determines the velocity of the portal, " Hermitaño explained.

"In the play, you wrote '*sesenta semanas dice que cocullen*' — in 'sixty weeks the Emmanuel will arrive.' Is the journey only sixty weeks?

"Not exactly. The sixty weeks I referred to is cosmic time, which is a fluid, spatial dimension with an infinite generation of movement in the fourth dimension." Hermitaño clarified.

"You hid the Portal of Light story for two millennia? How is that possible?" Pedro asked in amazement.

"Just as the *Ladino Hermanos* are able to conceal their story under the veil of Christianity, this original story of the birth of the Emmanuel was concealed within a brotherhood," Hermitaño said.

"You mentioned the word *Semano* — Heaven. Where was this heaven to these Ladino mystics?" Pedro asked.

"The Judaic mystics knew of a First Sun, Capricornus, located in the Capricorn Constellation. This first sun was four times the size of your current sun and over 8 billion years old. Other cultures such as Samarian and the Native American Hopi tribe were also aware of a concealed phenomena in our galaxy." Hermitaño illustrated with his hands lifting in a broad upward motion.

"What happened to this First Sun?"

"The First Sun became the location of *Semano* — Heaven. First Twin Sun imploded and collapsed, fusing hydrogen and helium after 8 billion years. This is called a supernova, creating a black hole, and then an enormous explosion of an entire section of the galaxy created the planets and moons that were blown in all directions to form the Milky Way galaxy," Hermitaño explained.

"This young galaxy formation was dry and lifeless, and yet the third planet from the new sun held together a fluid amniotic sack made of the rare Earth that floated in this part of the universe. This is called the *Firmamento* — Firmament, described in Genesis I and The Book of *Bereishit*-Torah."

> "And God said, Let there be a firmament in the midst of the waters, and let it divide the waters from the waters. And God made the firmament, and divided the waters which [were] under the firmament from the waters which [were] above the firmament: and it was so."

"Did the Higher Being God create this amniotic sack; how?" Pedro asked

"The Higher Being God has such advanced ability, that He knows how to use Dark Matter, an anti-gravitation matter, to pull with extreme gravitational force to create and separate the formation of cosmic bodies as clouds of cold gas, planets, comets, asteroids, stars, neutron stars, brown and white dwarfs and black holes," Hermitaño explained. "This is how the amniotic sack and the Portal of Light were created."

Artist Robert Maestas' 2015 drawing of the Cat's Eye Nebula

The Cat's Eye Nebula is an example of an antimatter controlled implosion of a star formation that is held together by anti-gravitational matter.

Our universe is composed of the non-visible and undetectable Dark Matter that comprises 73% of all matter and a separate 23% of Dark Energy within all matter. Both of these types of matter are the fabric that makes up most of the moving and static, non-moving energy fields that comprise our universe.

Pedro asked, "Tell us what artistry permits the Higher Being God to create the Portals?"

"The Higher Being God is capable of providing conscious directive that matter mold and design the creation of a fabric of intertwined Plank Strands that form the body of inertia for the purpose of travel to a distant constellation and the entry into another lower level dimension," the Hermitaño explained.

"So the Higher Being God manages matter behind a dark curtain that we cannot see?" Pedro queried.

"Yes, its operation is in a vastly higher dimension realm. Maybe 10 levels of dimensions above us on this earthly planet," Hermitaño said.

"The Portal is an invisible transparent membrane with a hollow core and whiplash strands that link on to one another, via low-lying magnetic nub spurs that hold together this transport of travel. The interlocking strands or strings of flowing movement act in conjunction with both dark and energy matter to create a supersonic velocity."

Then Pedro moved the topic from the scientific to the personal. "Tell us how the Higher Being God relates to regular people on Earth."

"The frontal lobe of the brain, or what you describe as the 'mind,' is where thoughts are received from the Higher Being God. It is here where the knowledge — conocimiento was originally stored by the Higher Being that made man and woman in their consciousness and earthly body," Hermitaño explained.

"Does the Higher Being God listen to the prayers of those who are his followers and pray to him?"

"The Higher Being is informed by both the conscious thought and prayer of those who are considered the faithful. He is acutely aware of his real followers, versus those who think they are real followers, for these are only fooling themselves if their values do not reflect the Word of the Lord that is written," Hermitaño explained.

"Will men and women in the future be able to manage matter with our conscious mind?" Pedro asked .

"Not immediately. The Higher Being God is a very ancient being. Your kind may be able to upgrade to the Fourth Dimension of working behind the curtain with dark matter and energy," Hermitaño explained.

The connection is a type of subliminal conversation of shared knowledge between the lowest-level communication of the Higher Being to the mind of the humble and open-minded man or woman who is open to this clairvoyant communication. The Higher Being God's advanced cerebral cortex and auditory nerve center are able to absorb thoughts and prayers of the most faithful because they share the same wavelength of telepathic communication. The human subconscious mind organically remembers the innate connection placed there by the Higher Being, the interface for both a conscious and spiritual relationship.

"A main lesson to remember is that one must 'walk the walk' of religious spirituality to connect to the Higher Being God. This does not fit everyone," Hermitaño said pointedly.

"How much of all of this were the ancient Judaic mystics aware of?" Pedro asked.

"In the play, the character Tubal, is grandson of Noah, and this is a clue to the historical nature of the anonymous Ladino writers of the play. These mystics passed down the calculation of velocity and the explanation of Time as primary keys to understanding of the Cosmos. These are the primary divulgence clues":

1. *Semano* — the Heaven and the distance in terms of light years to this nebula.
2. Understanding of the Dimension with Dark Matter and Dark Energy.
3. Velocity and Sound to determine capability of cosmic travel.
4. Time as Cosmic Time.

"Was Velocity a veiled clue in the play?" Pedro asked.

"Yes, the formula to determine the Velocity or the travel speed of Portal was disguised in the play. There are three clues that determine the location of the Ladino Heaven."

1. 1,000 is used in four separate occasions, to signify 1,000 to the 4th power.

   1,000 4th = 1 Trillion

2. Two in One Voice we go-"Dos en un Vos Bamos"

   Voice is cue for Sound

   Speed of Sound is 1,234 x Two = 2,468 per kilo hour

3. Beard or Whiskers of heaven - "*Barvaro de Semano*"

   Refers to visual constellation that possesses

   Whiskers: Capricorn

   Upper torso is man with beard, lower torso is a fish

Formula: 2,468 x 1,000 4th power = 2468 e 4th power or 2,468,000,000,000,000 Kilometers

Equivalent to the distance of 246 light years

"What Constellation is 246 light years from earth? Capricornus," Hermitaño answered.

The ancient mystics could 'eye locate' the constellation Capricornus. The last clue they provided for verification was a landmark corner. The star Dabih Major, located in the Capricorn star group, followed the latitude parallel line of the 33° North and is 1/6 from the corner point of the star assembly. It is the exact same place as the whiskers of the Sea Goat form of the constellation.

4. *"Un seis entre estos pastores"*-one-sixth between these shepherds.

The corner point of the Capricornus constellation and one-sixth from this point lies the whiskers of the face of the hybrid fish-human figure.

"It was the area of the Sun Capricornus on the constellation Capricorn, where the Judaic ancestral mystics knew their heaven was located," Hermitaño explained.

Waterton Canyon
Jefferson County, Colorado
Fall 2011

Antonio Encounters the Hermitaño

Antonio began his mountain bike trip up Waterton Canyon in the fall of 2011. The trail, while more of a pleasure ride, provided him with a picturesque Colorado canyon scenery at a slight incline, with the South Platte River roaring downward to fill Chatfield Reservoir to its limit. The red mountain bike and helmet were inconspicuous, as was Antonio, as he pushed up the trail to a specific location.

Upon arriving at the Mill Gulch bridge, halfway past the canyon to the Strontia Springs Reservoir, he noticed a man fishing from the bank of the river, dressed in a cowboy outfit and dark brown Stetson with tan hatband. The stranger watched Antonio as he dismounted from his bike, and then broke the silence. "You're on another thankless mission, I see. This time your package is under the waterfall."

Antonio stared at him, his brows almost knitted together. "And you, who are you?" he sneered as he took off his helmet.

"I know all about you. Today you will find a mini disc; hope it is not wet." Behind the two men, several white, sure-footed mountain goats stood mounted on the ridge on the other side of the trail. They stopped their climbing to take note of this tense situation and to watch what unfolded.

"You think you know something?" Antonio taunted. He moved slowly, like a dancer, down the embankment with his feet almost in plie position and his knees bent as he readied himself to pounce on this motherfucker. He quickly thought to himself, *a forearm to his left jugular and into the water he will go. What if he has the disc and it goes into the water?*

"Do you have the *cuaderno*? Have you figured out what Rubal meant?" The strange looking cowboy quizzed Antonio, causing him to pause and relax that attack stare that meant only one thing.

"You're dressed as a downtown cowboy, but who are you?" Antonio demanded, nodding his head upward. Yet, deep down, he realized only an insider would know about the disc and what *Rubal* meant.

"I am from your past; I come forward to share with you. I ask for nothing," the stranger replied. "Allow me to speak with you. Can we speak by the bridge, where there is shade?"

"You have 15 minutes!" Antonio shouted as he moved up the embankment and toward the bridge. The stranger reeled in his line and lifted his rod off the river, then followed Antonio to a shade tree.

Antonio sat on a dry, mossy rock. *This guy is off the water now, if I move on him quickly, he may have the disc,* he said to himself. The stranger sat across from him on a dry horizontal log and prodded his fishing pole upwards alongside of him. The crisp sound of the clean South Platte River culled by them, providing a soothing backdrop as two time frames were about to merge. Both looked intently at the other, the stranger as curious as Antonio, as the past encountered his future.

The Stranger spoke first. "I am from your past. I know all about you. I appeared in earnest for you since you come from a rural cowboy background. This is why I am dressed as so."

Anybody can don a cowboy outfit, Antonio thought. *Yet something is unparalleled; it is the fishing rod. The rod is a custom hexagon bamboo rod with the initials H.L Leonard at the shaft of the staff before it meets the cork handle that has an old fly and line connected to it. These rods are not used by amateurs. Americana at its best. Only the insiders can connect the moving water to the nature of fluency of the wood. The action of the cast by these rods is melded to the movement of the water, and they become as one. Only an authentic nature person uses these; only trainers of advanced Special Agents use these; only those who share intimate knowledge of how the world really works use these.*

"I am known as the Hermitaño" explained the stranger. "I am well-versed in your Judaic history, I know all that matters."

"Is this where you come from?" asked Antonio, *Are you real?* as he eyeballed every article of this person.

"I am an emissary. I help the Judaic people, and I will help your community, the Sephardim. You have been repressed for some time, but the Higher Being, God, listened to your subconscious prayers and pleas. Your timing of existence as a person in this time frame is what we want to work with," the Hermitaño said as he used his hands to explain the ending of the age of Pisces and the beginning of the age of Aquarius.

Antonio was aware of the changing of the ages along the Celestial Equator and asked, "You have arrived prior to the year of 2012, the beginning of the year of Aquarius."

"Correct. The play must be deciphered soon and shared during the 2012 year of Aquarius," the Hermitaño explained.

"For what purpose?"

"This will begin the sharing of the message, the coming of the Messiah. It is cloaked within the play."

"Why ask me to do this? You seem to think my efforts are thankless and not appreciated. What is the value to you?" Antonio reminded the stranger.

"That is why. You will be recognized as selfless in a world of selfishness. You are credible and trustworthy."

"You're an emissary, a messenger from the past. Why don't you do this?"

"Because I am not you. I am an outsider and not credible. I will not be believed even by you. And the many liberal Christians will not want to give you any credence."

"What makes you think I will do it?"

"You will. You must finish your mission as a Sephardim. You know this already. You used your skills to survive and conceal, this learned from the Kabbalists. Yet you will never receive recognition for your history or where your skills come from. Does this not bother you?"

Antonio looked closer at this stranger. His bronze skin glimmered in the sun as he made a valid point. Antonio was used to dealing with persons of faith, and one thing he learned is that persons in the crossroads of life come in all walks of life and skin color.

"Tell me your knowledge of this *cuaderno*?" Antonio asked.

"I landed in the time frame around 1732, a time of repression and unhappiness for the Sephardim. I befriended one of your *antipasado*-old family members and assisted him as he wrote the play you have in your hands. Pedro was his name, and he came from a Rabbinic family with a twist. The family escaped the noxious hands of the Inquisitors, caught up in flight to New Spain, yet this group had a separate understanding of the Cosmos, as well as a special knowledge of how to effectively hide for long durations of time."

"I know how to conceal myself and objects that I protect in plain sight," Antonio pointed out.

"Yet without my assistance, you cannot decode this play," the Hermitano explained. "It works like this:

"Special characters have a special purpose. *Lepio*, for example, links to the first sacking of Jerusalem in 583 B.C. You must recognize that the character *Lepido*, the Roman general that appointed Pontius Pilate to his position, is a historic Judaic figure. The same with *Tubal*, grandson of Noah. More depth of understanding of Judaic history is necessary. For example, when we placed two sentences from Flavius Josephus, you must be able to recognize these as clues. The word *Rubal*, this refers to *Rubal* al Khalid desert, the largest sand desert in all of Africa." The Hermitaño continued to divulge all of the clues of the play to consolidate this puzzle and the history of the Sephardim, known to themselves as Ladinos of New Spain.

"The *cuaderno* play came to you anonymously, and once deciphered, this play must be read by a small group in the year 2012."

"Why is this of importance?" Antonio asked.

"The reading of the decrypted code will signal a continuance of the age of Jesus of Nazareth, and this is of crucial importance to protect Christian and Judaic faith and culture. The values of persons of faith will be tested and challenged, and the reading of the code will extend the roots of the age of Pisces. The sharing of the birth of the Emmanuel will be enlightened by a Portal of Light."

"Nobody is familiar with this Portal of Light and an alternate birth story of Jesus of Nazareth," said Antonio.

"That is correct. That is why this story must reveal itself at the beginning of the age in 2012. You will complete a reading of the story at this beginning of the age of Aquarius. It will be up to you at a certain point to make the story public, either as a play or a book. Understand, few will accept your work or knowledge. Many Christians will berate your story as unrealistic, and even condemn it for not being in line with church teachings."

The Hermitaño stood up, lifted his rod, then walked up the embankment and disappeared. Antonio stayed a while longer, focusing on the rushing water. After collecting his thoughts, he rose to his feet, then scampered to the bridge, jumped and grabbed the cable, and swung through the waterfall without collecting a trace of water on his body. He searched for the package, a small, square, slender box adjoined to the cement inner wall behind the falls. There it was, just as the stranger had revealed. Antonio removed the plastic covering from the wall and looked at the package; it had not been compromised.

How did this Hermitaño guy obtain such secure information? Antonio wondered as he placed the package in his vest pocket and secured the button firmly. He only knew he must get this to his source immediately. He jumped back through the thick waterfall, picked up his helmet and rushed up the embankment. He turned his bike around, stepped on the forward pedal of his bike and returned down the trail to get in his truck.

On the way down the mountain, Antonio kept pondering: *Portal of Light and an alternate birth story of Jesus of Nazareth! Where did these concepts orginate?*

CHAPTER 3

The Hermitaño (1 BC)

Sheepherders Journey
Where: Sinai Mountain camp as journey begins
to meet the Emmanuel

The Hermitaño was invited to the main base camp of the shepherds, curious as to how this gardener appeared in this high altitude, caring for the meadow of carnations. Jila returned to her cooking area of stone rock shelving with a wire screen cook top. The fire starter of resin wood was used to start the fire to complete the *Migas* dish that she was preparing before departure.

The camp backed up against a small hill to prevent the high altitude's cool breeze from striking the fire. Large rocks and logs circled the encampment to provide protection against all adversaries that tried to challenge this group of faithful followers. Brush shrubs interlaced the foreground, providing the serenity and concealment to survive. Here, the shepherds gathered and sat down, looking inquisitively at the stranger as they waited for him to disclose himself.

Finally, the Hermitaño addressed them. "I arrive as a Time Traveler, a witness, to land in a different time frame — *venido a este rato* to view the Judaic community and observe their history. The time frames I have already encountered are the complete history of the Judaic community, and now I arrive along with the Emmanuel and will observe history from this prospective."

"You witnessed and lived in our history? For what reason?" Tubal queried.

"I am curious how this Messiah, the Child God, the Emmanuel, will change the perspective of mankind from this era of chaos you entered in 1 B.C. How will this child be accepted and treated? The future is what cannot be foretold in great detail. That is my purpose, to witness how this child-God is to be treated."

For a few seconds, the Hermitaño was lost in his own thoughts. *Little will mankind know of the Emmanuel's advanced mental and healing capabilities, as he will live as a commoner, wearing a human sack cloth of skin — ropa del piel.*

"You are able to see and feel what will happen to this child?" Tubal asked.

"Yes, a first-hand observation of history, beginning with his birth," Hermitaño detailed.

Hermitaño was aware that these shepherds were on the cusp of witnessing a rare event that would stop time. It was an exciting event for the Hermitaño to join the human sheepherders as they gathered their flock and made ready for the journey. The shepherds naturally accepted him as one of their own and understood that he was deeply knowledgeable about their Judaic faith. This journey and the life of the Emmanuel would be reported to the Higher Being God as a witness.

"Explain to us how the Higher Being stays connected to mankind?" Jila asked.

Hermtaño answered, "Interestingly, on our plane, communication is carried out telepathically. But the real in-depth sharing of knowledge, music, and philosophy is completed through prayer or meditation. This knowledge from both the conscious prayer state and the non-conscious prayer state is received telepathically from the Higher Being."

"We are not aware of this," Jila said.

"Amazingly, mankind has yet to figure out that their existence derives from their consciousness. Let me explain this to you. The Higher Being placed thought and memory into your physical bodies to assist in mankind's development into evolved humans. The strands of Plank placed in the prefrontal vortex lobe has developed the conscious mind to think independently, as well as to speak coherently, to evaluate, reason and plan," he explained.

"What is plank?" Jila asked.

"Plank is the invisible, conscious strand links in the brain that permits higher analytical thought. The ability to create is one example," Hermitaño answered.

"It still amazes me that you cannot recognize this. It is as if you need a tangible, real-life figure to provide proof that there is a Higher Being."

You expect us to understand a conscious mind or recognize the value that a High Being God provides? Jila pondered to herself.

"The Higher Being God provides the spirituality that is perceived as a mystery. Being a shepherd in the Sinai, you are aware of this spiritual existence. The meaning for the arrival of the Messiah is that God is with us," the Hermitaño explained.

Prior to his arrival through the Portal of Life, the Hermitaño lived happily in a different form in the dimension of *Semano* — Heaven in the galaxy of Capricornus. His physical figure resembled that of a dolphin. His conscious thinking mind existed many centuries happily on the other side of Dark Matter. Living in a world where oxygen need not exist, he survived. There, the empty space of the cosmos was his home, where he was able to communicate telepathically with the Higher Being.

The dolphin figure maintained a large corpus callosum — the nerve center of the brain that connects two separate cerebral cortexes — whereas humans maintain only one small cortex. One side is able to shut down sleep and the other side stay awake, and then reverse them so that the brain is constantly functioning. Then the larger auditory advanced nerve center is placed next to the cortex that permits rapid response to sounds heard or felt.

It was one of these highly conscious beings that the Higher Being God called to make this all-important journey to Earth at this time.

The Hermitaño, as he was later to be known by select humans, had been prepared by learning about the history, music, economics and social issues within his journey's location. Since his specialty was Judaic history, he had served more than once in assisting suppressed Jews, attired in his human sack — *ropa de piel* — upon arrival on Earth. Upon termination of the sack cloth body, his spirit and consciousness elevate and join the conscious that exists in the earthly world.

Tubal interrupted, "Help me comprehend this. An advanced civilization exists behind Dark Matter — the Dark Curtain — and created a mechanism to travel light years in length at astounding speed to visit mankind that has been made in the Higher Being God's conscious image. Then He enlightened the sky with this Portal of Light so we shepherds, who have been awaiting this sign, can then follow it to the birthplace of the Emmanuel?

"Yes, it is a very special journey."

"Tell us about this mechanism that has this ability to travel," Jila raised her palms out, trying to understand this technology.

Hermitaño described the travel vehicle to Tubal and Jila. "The strands that moved this Portal exhibit the most advanced Plank Energy Propulsion system, a sustainable solar matrix of Dark Energy Matter that acquired solar energy by means of the invisible Plank Strands' fluid movement. The result is the movement of an energy field into the Portal of Light that navigated within the vast field of the cosmos to encompass the Multi-Universe at travel speeds beyond the speed of light. This is the most advanced form of travel mechanism ever created, and not all civilizations spend their resources to have this ability."

"Where does this journey begin?" Jila asked.

"The journey began in *Semano* — the Ladino word for Heaven. *Barbudos de Semano* — Beard of Heaven — refers to the Ladino location of Heaven, the whiskers in the Capricornus constellation.

Located in the Southern Hemisphere of our Milky Way's galaxy, it is home to our Twin Star, a now dwarf star that was the original light of creation that bore the light to create the dry universe of no water or life. This Twin Star is over 8 billion years of age, twice the age and twice the size of your current sun star. It once dominated the Milky Way galaxy," Hermitaño added.

"Why can't we see this heaven?" Jila asked.

"The Higher Being God derived from a dimension that humans are unable to perceive. The Higher Being is not a physical, tangible figure and would be best understood as a conscious presence. The Higher Being God placed the ability to think consciously in human beings as a figurative parallel to 'His Image.' The Higher Being-God is not a tangible figure, but functions within the field of undetectable Dark Matter, which permeates the universe and, therefore, is never tangibly seen," the Hermitaño explained.

"Why not a tangible image so that humans can look and say, 'There! There is God, himself, standing?" Jila asked.

Hermitaño shot back immediately, "The Higher Being God does not possess a physical image and does not function in only one singular dimension, as do humans. Your consciousness exists on both a spiritual and supraliminal level. The supraliminal level is a higher conscious plane and this is parallel to where the *Semano* — Heaven was derived. To be able to operate at this separate conscious level of a higher plane of a 4th Dimension, one needs the ability to view all sides of matter at once, and this is when you will realize and understand that God exists and is not a physical, tangible being, but pure consciousness."

"Is this the murmur that I feel when praying or in a spiritual trance? Jila asked.

Hermitaño answered, "Yes, the light and conscious can be extracted in this manner. This is why the Higher Being God placed your consciousness behind your forehead — *frente* — since this is the most accessible location for the Higher Being God to connect with."

"Your story sounds as though you must conceal yourself after all of these years. Is there a time in the future when this community must hide themselves as well?" Tubal asked.

"Yes, there will be a lengthy period prior to when the alternative story of the birth of Jesus of Nazareth is shared. The Sephardim or *Seraditas*, as they are known in a new territory and community, will be repressed for some time and be required to conceal themselves," The Hermitaño explained.

"Can you tell us of this repression and how they concealed themselves?" Jila asked.

CHAPTER 4

1840, The Great Veil of Concealment

Las Mujeres — **The Women**
**The adobe home-*casita* of Jila, her brother Pedro
and the Hermitaño near Chupadero, New Mexico**

The Ladino women were an integral component of both maintaining and concealing the Judaic faith within their families. Maintaining the faith was linked to the care and customs provided around the province of the women's home.

Jila was visiting the town market in Chupadero and noticed a man selling curious herbs and plant resins on a small table with a white cloth — *mantel* that covered the entire area of the facia of the table. Jila noticed something unique on the table, *Yerba Buena*-mint, but this was not your typical mint that was used for cures of insect bites, swollen gums, and mouthwash. What Jila noticed was the full white bloom still attached to the plant. She had not seen this since her mother taught of the use of the bloom.

"Que ese so — what is that," she asked the man.

"That is *Yerba Buena* — Good Herb" the man answered.

"No, I mean the white blossom? The blossom, not sure, what would you use that for? My mother used the blossom, not sure for what ailment," Jila answered.

"The flat leaf is oily and used for medicinal purposes, the white flower contains the seed and is slender. Used to cure pinworms," the man said.

"Yes, that is what I remember. For those people kept in caves or moist areas get these bugs. Few know this remedy," Jila observed.

"Tell me, your *mantel* is full of cures, many not seen or used in this area with commonality. Are you from this area? Jila asked. She had recognized the knowledge of the Ladino vendor.

"Yes, my roots are from here, many a time now," the man said.

"I have to continue my day. Could you stop by my casita in the early evening? I live not too far from here. *Mi nombre es Jila* — my name is Jila" as she introduced herself and wrote on paper directions to her adobe.

"I will, we may have much in common. I am the Hermitaño."

The Hermitaño arrived in the early evening at the adobe home of Jila. His purpose was to understand the role of the Ladino women in this time period. He arrived at the home and knocked on the door. Jila opened the door and introduced her brother Pedro, who was visiting at this time. They all sat in the *salsa* — living room.

"Jila, is it possible for you to prepare kosher foods? The Hermitaño surprisingly asked.

"It is possible to prepare kosher meals and traditions, but it is just that we do not have certain ingredients to prepare such meals and have to resort to use other means to complete the same meal," Jila replied as she felt a calm and safety speaking with this stranger.

Hermitaño was curious about this. "Can you give me an example?"

Jila thought and said, "Do you know *Capriatada*? This is a very popular bread pudding, baked with dry or moistened bread. But we use unsalted soda crackers as the unleavened substitute and it tastes just as good. We eat this on Passover in early April since it coincides with Easter. I also like to use greens on the day of Passover, so we use the wild spinach called *quelites*. These are prepared with onion, salt, soda crackers and steamed over the fire. We call this *migas*, and it's quite tasty."

"Hmmm. Interesting," Hermitaño responded.

"It is best to coincide holiday foods with each other. I make *Torte Huevo*, a staple food during the Lenten period of April and make this continuously during the Passover period," Jila added.

"What is *Torte Huevo*?" Hermitaño asked.

"*Torte Huevo* is separating the egg whites and beating into a batter. We then crumble the unleavened soda crackers into a patty and fry it in oil on both sides, then add the egg batter back into the skillet and this forms a flat patty. That is folded back in the yellow yokes and cooked on both sides." Jila explained. "This must be served with red chili and no meat during Lent. If not, it is a giveaway that you are cooking in a style that is not Catholic. Eaten with a flat flour tortilla, this is our unleavened bread.

"Where did you learn this from?" the Hermitaño asked.

"*Mi mama* — my mother," Jila answered fondly.

"Your home is well-kept and clean. I notice white linens over the furniture."

Jila proudly explained, "It is our Sabbath day of rest. I will light candles or start the fire before sundown. We must be careful; this is one of the main Judaic practices that will be reported to the priest by Christian visitors." Hermitaño asked, "What would the priest do with this information?

"He will report us to the Holy Office of the Inquisition in Santa Fe, and they will begin an investigation as possible heretics. We must also not wear white clothes on the Sabbath, a clear give-away of who we are," Jila, said firmly.

"I notice you have Santos on your *cómoda* — bureau. This is unusual for a Judaic family."

"Unusual maybe, but definitely necessary. All families have Santos, or *bultos*, in their homes. We have St. Esther, the Catholic saint for the Sephardim, but not everyone knows this. Purim, the holiday to commemorate their Judaic salvation, celebrates the book of Esther, which is celebrated in mid-March of each year. I may make unleavened cookies. We also have a Judaic Crucifix. Ever seen one of these?" She pointed to the wall.

"No, I have not. Are the, are those Santos actually prayed to?" Hermitaño asked looking for clarity.

"No, but sometimes you may get caught up in a group prayer that Catholics like to do here. We may have a Santo in our hand, but we are consciously praying to Moses."

"How is all of this information shared? Hermitaño asked.

Jila, laughed, "Haircuts! I give most of the haircuts to most of the women, our *comadres*, and to the young children in this village. I educate, inform and then share holiday updates. The older *comadres* bring me important communication that must be shared with the men."

"What type of important communication?" Hermitaño quizzed.

Jila paused and thought, then said, "If the priest or inquisitors are to be visiting our area, if any of the Católicos are asking questions about our families, or if any of our Judaic customs have been recognized, or when the *Morada* will be safe to share a religious service."

Puzzled, Hermitaño interjected, "Yet all of this happens while at the same time you participate in their Christian services?"

"Yes" Pedro said, "Our weddings, for example."

"Did you use the gift of coins during the wedding?" the Hermitaño surmised.

"Yes, by use of the wedding custom called *La Entrega de los Novios*, a New Mexican Lasso ceremony to signify unity in the marriage," Pedro answered.

"How does this work?"

"A large rosary of beads is wrapped around the sitting couple. This was borrowed from the Native American tradition where they wrap a blanket around the couple to signify their union. Coins were then tossed upon a blanket by the community at the feet of the couple to fulfill the *Act of Kinyan*. The coins tossed on the blanket signify the value the groom brings to the nuptials. "Shouts of '*Que viva los novios* — Long live the married couple,' are heard in the background."

Shaking his head, Hermitaño pondered out loud, "And nobody notices this as a Judaic practice?"

"No, this was the gift of choice from the community," Pedro answered.

"Did the groom prepare a home for the bride before the marriage?" Hermitaño asked.

"Yes, the adobe was built and purchased prior to the wedding," Pedro quipped.

"Very Judaic!" Hermitaño observed with a smile.

The adobe home — *casita* of Jila, her brother Pedro and the Hermitño near Chupadero, New Mexico

The Life of the *Seraditas* — Sephardim

"Tell me, Pedro, how are you able to conceal yourselves?" The Hermitaño asked.

"It began with the Ladino language, the hybrid Hebrew and Spanish dialect of the Seraditas, or Sephardim that many considered the old archaic Castilian Spanish. This formed as a written language after the onset of the Inquisition in 1492. Prior to that time, it was only an oral language. But when our ancestors brought it to New Spain, we continued to use it among ourselves to conceal our history in written form. This Ladino language has influenced every aspect of life in this territory. Ladino and formal Castilian Spanish are pronounced the same; only the written forms are different from one another. From there, concealment practices became more complex. An example is the name of my sister Jila. It is a passed-down family name, a name that derives from the book of Daniel. Most people do not know this."

Jila continued, "For Ladino families, fasting was abstaining from food or drink and was an act of maintaining their commitment to both their Christian and Judaic faiths. The Ladinos imposed these penances upon themselves to expiate their sins in an outward adherence to the rules of the Roman Catholic Church, while simultaneously serving as a penance within their Judaic faith."

"For example, fasting," Pedro explained, "was prevalent not only as expiation for sins, but also as an expression of thanks to the Lord for deliverance from the Holy Office of the Inquisition. Living as a Jew and concealing our Judaic faith created a horrendous hardship for anyone living as a dual-faith person. Fasts were observed openly by stating they were in honor of the Virgin Mary or Carmen (Nuestro Señora de Carmen, under this title, mother Mary is patron to the Carmelite Order) when they were, in fact, done to expiate sins or as a request for deliverance from evil, such as their discovery and arrest by the Inquisition. The fast actually occurred on the special days of Yom Kippur, *El Gran Día de Ayuno* — The Great Day of Fast, and *El Día De Perdón* — The Day of Pardon, and typically would last one day."

Jila continued, "The fast for Purim Ta'anit Ester — The fast for Esther — typically lasted from sunrise to sunset. The Ladino community related to Esther's purpose of gathering fortitude from fasting because she fasted for three days prior to revealing to her husband, King Ahashueros, her true identity as a Jewess, to prevent the slaughter of her fellow Jews by Haman. This was an example for Ladinos to imitate to uphold their lives as cryptic Jews."

"So you have been fasting at the same time for two different events?" Hermitaño asked.

"Yes," Jila replied. "Fasting for Catholic days of Obligation also means fasting for a secondary Judaic purpose. Although the dates of the Catholic and Judaic days of observation never match exactly, the Ladino community dedicated the closest day possible to observe their special days. The day of Purim, the Fast Day of Esther in early

March or late February, was observed on the Catholic day of Ash Wednesday. Fasting for Holy Week in early April often dovetails to the beginning of Passover — *Pesach*. Ladinos abstaining from foods on the Catholic Feast Day of Assumption in mid-August was remembrance of Yom Kippur that many times begins in mid-September."

"How would Ladinos be able to recognize that another Ladino was fasting?" Hermitaño asked.

Pedro eyes opened wide and he said, "The use of toothpicks in mouth while outside in the community was the deception sign that they had just eaten. It was a subterfuge for their fasting days among the Ladino families. If a toothpick could not be located, a piece of a strand from the straw of the broom would also be used. Others claimed stomach illness or sleeping during meals. This technique used to deceive servants or outsiders for Ladinos not eating meals during a lengthy fast."

"Interesting. Still no verbal communication. What about at home?" Hermitaño quizzed.

"The Ladinos identified their concealed internal fasting to other Ladino families by the use of candles that were put out prior to or during the fasting period so as to be accepted as a normal Catholic religious tradition. Remember, all homes at this time only used candles for light in the evenings," Jila noted.

"This act of spiritual commitment also provided a camouflage for Jews, as the Spanish Catholic community would never question the faith of any person who was fasting as a spiritual practice," Pedro explained.

"We would then begin the process for the preparation for prayer. Bathing the day before and use of new or clean shirts and dresses was an absolute must. Dining on fish and vegetables was common. The only fish available were small trout from a nearby river or lake. Eggs were also common; *torte huevo* was my favorite. We paid our nephew for a freshly caught creek trout. This was a common practice," Jila explained.

"At home we would have a small group of friends meet for the prayer session. Living in very secluded rural areas, with neighboring homes sometimes up to a mile away, provided the seclusion and privacy to conduct private services with small groups of two to five family members or close-knit friends who would meet to share prayers," Pedro explained.

"Meeting on the special days of Yom Kippur or *El Día de Perdón* — the Day of Pardon, the Ladino groups would meet and recite prayers until after midnight, sometimes staying overnight. Children would be sent to sleep around nine o'clock in the evening. These events would not become rituals that the outside Catholic community would notice a pattern or wonder what is going on within any particular home. Rather, it would just be an infrequent gathering among friends and relatives who arrived to have a good, long visit," Jila explained.

Pedro picked up the topic of how they actually prayed together. "One of the most common and safe readings was the Book of Wisdom from Solomon, known in both the Torah and in the Old Testament. A source of consolation, study and as a prayer, the Ladinos could openly use this material in a spiritual and happy manner for its use in Hebrew and Christian traditions. We also prayed the Shema, (Deuteronomy 6:14), *Hear, O Israel: The LORD our God, the LORD is one. You shall love the LORD your God with all your heart and with all your soul and with all your might.*"

"Were the traditional prayers normally used in these settings?" Hermitaño asked.

"Not entirely," Pedro explained. "It was not unusual that prayers for protection were said to provide calm and protection for the Ladino community." In *Psalm 17* or *Tehillim 7* of the Orthodox Jewish Bible, this Prayer of David reads:

"Keep me as the apple of Your eye;
Hide me under the shadow of Your wings,
From the wicked who oppress me,
From my deadly enemies who surround me."

"Tell me, were any Catholic and Judaic hybrid prayers created?"
Hermitaño asked.

"The constant and close interaction of the historical Jews and
Catholics produced new hybrid rites. Many Jews from the Iberian
peninsula learned from Spanish Catholics that suffering and self-
denial were a means to salvation. Ladinos fasting for Holy days
of Obligation also meant devout prayer for the secondary Judaic
days of observation of Yom Kippur that was acknowledged by the
Judaic calendar in the month of September or later. The actual
day acknowledgments do not have to be exact; the importance is the
prayer and fast for a specific holiday that is important. Also, the
actual day is not discernible since it is based on the lunar calendar
many times," Pedro explained

"Were prayers then commingled?" Hermitaño asked.

"Yes, the Christian prayers were often written with Ladino words,
cryptic Judaic religious concepts and philosophy. This influence
deepened the spirituality of the Ladino community in the people of
this territory," Pedro explained.

"How was this done? Would this not be a giveaway of their
Judaic faith?" Hermitaño was still skeptical.

"They often did it within the songs of praise, the *Alabados*" Pedro
said.

"Within the *Morada*, the little chapel?"

"Yes, it was the only way." Pedro said. "The Hermandad had always tried to protect the Christian faith within their community, and
so one thing they did was to maintain their perennial customs during
Passion Week. This was the only way to be discreet and yet spiritually
connect to our ancestral faith," Pedro explained.

"Is this not a type of spiritual slavery?

"The depth of understanding and importance of the law of Moses becomes even more relevant. The spirituality is not enslaved. The knowledge provided by our Lord is the in-depth clarity of the understanding of the scripture and the advanced esoteric wisdom of the universe," Pedro explained.

"I sense that the private prayers were sacred or secret," The Hermitaño asked.

"Yes," Jila answered. "The Friars from the Inquisition identified both heretic families and friends by linking their private prayers with the forced extracted prayers from other family members. Hence, the private prayers become confidential and sacred for survival."

"The *Alabados* are sung many times after lighting the candles or the Menorah. This is when the *Ladino Hermanos* would share their esoteric wisdom of the cosmos and the Portal of Light with each other," Pedro explained.

"The *Ladino Hermanos* and their families never disclosed Ladino-influenced *Alabados* or *The Portal of Light* story," Jila added.

"Who was this shared with?"

"The esoteric and cosmic information known only to the *Ladino Hermanos de Luz* — Brothers of Light was considered sacred, and this was only shared among themselves," Pedro explained.

"The *Hermanos de Luz* maintained the cosmic knowledge, the study of the stars and the Portal of Light. I understand why it was maintained in this confidential manner," Hermitaño observed.

Pedro added, "Yes, yet even in the repressed venues, spirituality and faith grows. I would not call it a Spiritual Slavery. There is but One Faith."

"How do you expect to sustain yourselves?" The Hermitaño asked.

1840 New Mexico
The New Arrivals

"We sustain ourselves by new arrivals." Pedro added.

"What new arrivals?" Hermitaño asked.

"Jila, show him the list and how we operate with the newcomers. We are shared of the new arrivals to the community by either Ladino families that send their *primos* — cousins to this area or other Ladino persons that are aware of all those entering the area," Pedro explained

Jila reached to the slim hiding place in the cupboard below the board lining and removed the list. Plainly, she stated, "We are always informed when a new family has arrived or is going to be arriving to this area. The list includes our internal notes of the details of the families and if we can possibly include them within our private services. Here, let me show you," she said, pointing to one name, "a new family will arrive soon.

"The father is Católico and the mother Judaic. They have three children and will arrive in May. We do not know if we can share the cryptic story with this family; therefore, we will get to know them before offering the play to them."

She moved her finger down to another name and said, "A second Gallegos family has also arrived. They have five children, some of them with red hair. Both parents are Judean, the youngest can see. So we need to take the Jornado play to them soon and ask them to join the *Morada*.

"A third Martinez family has arrived. He is Judaic, the wife is not. Be careful of the wife; she is Católica, related to the brothers in the *Hermandad*. She thinks she knows much but is only a foot soldier for the church. Be careful here."

"How do you know which persons you can share the cryptic story with?" Hermitaño asked.

"First of all, you must have some knowledge of Judaic history, a holiday, a certain way prayers are read, a knowledge of the way food is prepared, something that lets a witness know you are Ladino. From here you are examined to see if you can share in our knowledge," Jila explained.

"*Can see.*" Hermitaño repeated. What do you mean here?"

Jila answered, "It is very rare to have the ability to comprehend the knowledge of the mystics, to speak other languages and to possess a certain level of clairvoyance. A person of the land, who works with the land, gets along well with the *indigenes* — indigenous people in this territory."

"I have seen this before. The old monarchs of Spain used the Jewish administrators to run the kingdom while the Christians fought the Moors in Spain. The court could never figure out how the Jewish administrators were so skilled at their jobs. Finally I asked how they did it. I was told they 'could see' events and negotiations before they began and were able to then complete these tasks with great expedience," The Hermitaño said.

"That is essentially our experience. They do not appear often," Jila replied.

"You see," Pedro added, "the list will provide families for our continued existence."

"Or your demise. All it takes is one person to share with their spouse their historic family background," Hermitaño warned.

"They have been informed, and know it is not wise or safe for them to do so," Jila chimed in.

"You mentioned a play?" Hermitaño then asked.

"Our Ladino community shares a play called the *Jornado de Exódo* — *The Journey of Exodus*. It is a cryptic play that conceals words for Hebrew and Ladino, laced with the sentences and concepts from ancient writers, such as Homer and Flavius Josephus. The character names reflect Judaic history markers and much more," Jila answered.

"How is this shared?" the Hermitaño questioned.

Pedro responded, "When we are certain that a person or family is committed to their Judiac faith, we share the play with them or when we have prayer sessions.

Hermitaño noticed, "You said 'a person or family'?" Hermitaño asked.

Jila explained, "Sometimes only one spouse is Judaic, and the other is Católico."

Hermitaño's curiosity piqued, "Then only one part of the couple will pass down their heritage," he said. You Spanish Sephardim are interesting — so audacious. I have seen acts of faith, but the Lord will acknowledge your faith sevenfold some day!

Pedro then said, "Let us go back to the *Morada*. They are doing repairs today and the other *Ladino Hermanos* will be there too."

Pedro and the Hermitaño arrived by horse at the remote location of the *Morada*. They stopped as they viewed an interesting feud going on as they paused at an overlooking ridge.

On this particular day, Pedro and the Hermitaño arrived to view a challenge of land and faith between two parties that sought existence. The interchange was between the existing culture and faith of the native inhabitants, likely of a Jicaria-Apache tribe, and the recently arrived immigrants, who were Spanish Catholics. This is best shown in a play format to be able to view the nuances of each culture.

1840
Village of Chupadero and their Morada
North of present-day Santa Fe, New Mexico

The *Morada* of *Chupadero* held historic importance for the small community outside of Santa Fe, New Mexico. At one point in history prior to the mid 1840s, this small chapel was the central location for religious services within the Spanish Catholic community. This was before the establishment of large adobe churches and places of services used by the friars and priests to serve this community.

Now in the 1840s New Mexico territory, prior to the arrival of American colonialism and the hope of what capitalism would possibly bring to the area, the *Morada* provided both the preservation of spirituality and religious customs in a land that lacked any formal Christian theological formation. Individuals and families attended services in the small *Morada* chapels, prior to the time of religious formation within structured church settings that were brought later into this territory.

To the cryptic Ladino community, the *Morada* was still the only sacred place where Judaic group services could be performed in relative safety. It was always a truly sacred place where the smooth adobe walls welcomed and absorbed prayers from all comers, regardless of their faith. The walls were hand-laid by both Christian and Ladino Hermano Penitente brothers who massaged the earth-bound mud from their hearts for their faith in a Lord. Mother earth responded to this love with her brown and red mud of *cariño* — caring that absorbed all who speak and sing to her.

To the Judaic community that lived in Chupadero, participation in the Hermandad became a lifetime commitment, for they understood its importance. Throughout this territory, Ladino members of the Hermandad became the caretakers of the sacred adobe sanctuary, *La Morada*, unknown by the leaders of the *Morada*, los *Hermanos* Mayor. Whenever the roof needed fixing, floor repaired, window replaced, altar renovated, or Santos moved, it was one of the skillful Judaic *Hermanos*, known among themselves as the *Ladino Hermanos*, who would step up for this assignment, for they knew that this sacred place was the only safe place for them to meet.

The *Morada*s were typically located in a place that you cannot easily find, for the *Hermandad* preferred privacy. An adobe building made of 12-by-12- inch handmade bricks stacked three foot in width typically built for three rooms and built by members of the *Hermanos Penitentes*. The larger of the three rooms was used for prayer recital and singing the *Alabados*.

This large room typically contained a cast-iron stove with a chimney reaching up to the roof where the sweet smell of piñon wood would create the incense into the rooms that lay upon one's breath and within their throat to never leave your memory. The second room is where altars were constructed and initially wood carvings of various saints and prayer beads would be on display. And for the *Ladino Hermanos*, the usage of the Bench — *La Tribunal* was common.

The last small room was the entry way where coats were hung and boots left red clay and mountain dirt upon the rough hardwood pine planks. The roof typically was held up by *vigas* or peeled, round cross logs that supported the entire roof.

The interior of the *Morada* maintained a darker soot color on the walls above the cast-iron stove, which released heat and smoke that tarnished the partition and logs. The few windows were aligned to midway to balance each room with the outside of the adobe exterior and were typically fortified with shutters on the inside to keep the *Morada* safe when not in use. The 3-inch-thick doors were made of wide pine planks that can withstand any type of weather condition and provided the strength of solitude that the Brotherhood required. The furniture usually consisted of long benches made of pine wood, where the *Hermanos* sat to sing *Alabados* or recite prayers together.

There was no physical difference between a Spanish Catholic *Hermano* and a Ladino *Hermano*, and never was there ever any acknowledgement of prayers, *dichos* — sayings or knowledge among the *Ladino Hermanos* to show that they were of any different background than the Spanish Catholics. To disclose any inkling of Judaic history in this deeply spiritual Christian environment could easily cost the Ladino Hermano his life and that of the others he would be forced to disclose. Yet all of this was worth the risk for the single opportunity to have a sanctuary where the Judaic faith could survive.

The *Morada* Visited by Native Warriors

*The delicate nature of this section requires
a play format to share this story.*

[Inside the *Morada*]

Juan: I thought you said no one could find the *Morada*, but I see three horses in the distance.

Jose: Those are Indians!

Ramon: What kind of horses are those? They look like Palominos.

Juan: Small Palominos, Pedro. You sold those in the Taos trade fair two springs ago to a *Jircaria*-Apache fellow! It is misty outside. Maybe they will just pass by.

Ramon: They are dressed for war! They have bows, and they are wearing stripes across their faces and legs. This is not a civil event for them.

Jose: How was I supposed to know? I sold them small horses, but we still have our large Arabes!

Juan: You are going to lose your scalp! Just for a few dollars! We need to sing, *Canta Jondo* and loud!

Let us sing *Santo Madero* and make it loud so they think there are many singing

> "Bendito el Santo Madero
> Arbol de la Santa Cruz
> Dondi fuimos dedimos"

[Native Warrior band]

Chinche: Do they see us? How many are there? That is not a house. What is it?

Two Coyote: It is not a house. There is nowhere to hang clothes, no chickens, no goats.

Chinche: I have heard of these adobe houses where strange sounds come from. I think the *Españoles* do their worship service here. It's a prayer house.

Two Coyote: I can now hear them singing. What kind of singing is that?

Chinche: Listen, slow and lonely. Sounds like they're crying. Where does this music come from? Our music is much better; bet they can't even dance.

Two Coyote: Do we attack?

Chinche: There are many singing. Yet I only see three horses.

Conejo Feo: I will dismount. I think I see a big head sticking out from the window.

[Return to the *Morada*]

Ramon: Keep singing. They have stopped and are just looking. Do we approach them?

Juan: No, keep singing. Ramon, what do you see? (Juan continues singing.)

> Bendito el Santo Madero
> Arbol de la Santa Cruz
> Donde fuimos redimos…

Ramon: [Pokes head outside wood window frame]
> I see three horses, and the men are dismounting.
> They are behind those big rocks, up the hill.

[Return to Native Warrior Band]

Chinche: Conejo Feo, can you shoot with your arrow?

Conejo Feo: Yes.

Chinche: Go around to the right, duck down and get an angle around the boulder. Take the shot. Two Coyotes, go with him . . . be very quiet.

Two Coyotes: Here, stop. Take the shot at the big head in the open square.

Conejo Feo: O.K. Here goes . . . Damn it! Ooooh! (grieving in pain)

Chinche: What happened?

Two Coyotes: He shot his foot.

Chinche: What? What am I going to tell your mother, my sister? You stupid ass!

Two Coyotes: He slipped on the wet peyote leaf and marijuana plants. As he let go, the bow went down and his foot went up, and he shot himself.

Chinche: That is why they will never allow smoking marijuana and peyote in these lands. Our Medicine men do that and they sleep 'til noon and wake with their stories of visions and dancing in the air with bald eagles, and seeing white buffalo that are not in this mountain area, while we get to do all of the work around the camp. Our elders believe these stories and send us to hunt deer or steal some chickens or goats from the Espanoles. And we end up shooting ourselves in the foot!

Two Coyotes: What do we do? They know we are here; they have rifles.

[Return to the *Morada*]

Pedro: What do you see, Ramon?

Ramon: I see three Indians. One is on the ground. Sounds like he is crying.

Jose: Crying!! That's the native war cry! What do we do? We only have our *pistolas* — pistols.

Juan: Keep singing. It is working. The power of our *Alabados*!

Ramon: No! No! The one on the ground has an arrow through his foot!

Juan: You shot him with an arrow? You have a pistol, you *pendejo*! — stupid!

Ramon: Maybe he shot himself? Can he be that dumb? I've done some dumb things before.

[Native Warrior Band]

Chinche: Pick Conejo Feo up and put him on his horse. The elders will never believe this story.

Two Coyotes: Let's tell them we ran into Comanches from Taos, who were raiding the same *Españoles*. We battled for the same home, and they shot at us!

Chinche: I made the arrow, Stupid! They will figure out who made the arrow. You want to tell them you slipped on a peyote plant, and the arrow magically went into your foot? You have been hanging out with the medicine men!! Smoking Peyote! Let's get out of here! Look who they send me out with (he murmurs).

[Return to the *Morada*]

Jose: That was close. But they are leaving now. Wonder who shot his foot.

Ramon: Maybe the holy winds from our *Alabados* in the air returned the arrow into his foot.

Juan: You are a *pendejo* — stupid. Let me tell you now!

Jose to the other *Hermanos*: "Let's plan to meet in two weeks after Mass."

All *Hermanos* inside the *Morada* mount their horses and leave.

[Return to steep incline, where Pedro and the Hermitaño had been observing]

Hermitaño observed the entire scenario and comments, "Boy, these are certainly not the ones that 'can see.' Isn't there a vaquero training school that these lads can go to?"

Pedro confessed, "Unfortunately, these are not the sharpest knives in thechuckwagon."

Hermitaño asked, "And the native ones are your mighty adversaries? Have you thought about asking them to join up with you? Kind of the same cloth, if you know what I mean."

Pedro sighs, "Oy Vey."

"I see a Menorah in the window, on top of the altar," Hermitaño excitedly observed.

The *Ladino Hermanos* introduced the *Menorah* candle into the *Morada* at the inception of the establishment of the Hermandad. Since *Moradas* typically do not have use of any external lighting, the use of candles and the *Menorah* can be the primary nighttime source of light. To the *Ladino Hermanos*, the nine-branch candelabrum is the remembrance that links historically to the Hanukah holiday, which commemorates the Jewish recapture and rededication of the Temple in Jerusalem in 164 B.C.

"How was the *Menorah* used by the Christian *Hermanos*?"
Hermitaño asked.

"In the common public ceremonies with both Christian and
Ladino Hermanos, most ceremonies' use of the Menorah was only
for Christian rituals." During Holy Week on Holy Thursday, 14
candles are put out, one by one, as the Stations of the Cross were
conducted. As each station is completed, one candle is blown out
until the very last candle is extinguished and total darkness encom-
passes the *Morada*. This signifies the death of Christ.

The Hermitaño asked, "And what of the private ceremonies of
the *Ladino Hermanos*?"

Pedro answered, "That is different. The Menorah and candles
were used in short, secret ceremonies for the major holidays, such as
Yom Kippur, Passover and definitely Purim, in remembrance of St.
Esther. Also, in the play the *Jornado de Exódo* — Journey of Exodus
sections would be read and shared among the *Ladino Hermanos*."

Hermitaño commented, "Using the Menorah as a symbol of importance to both Christian and Judaic faith is fascinating. Maybe
this holds value for the future of both faiths working together."

Pedro continued, "The Menorah candelabra, at home, has more
specific Judaic links. The Menorah was placed upon a clean white
cloth, and this was placed upon the floor so no one from the outside
would see the candles lit. Then kneeling to do individual prayers was
common in a home, such as the *Song of Moses*, Exodus 15:1 or *Psalm
23* by David in Torah. A special prayer, thought and reverence for
the story of Esther and her Sephardic story relates notably with the
Sephardic people in this territory."

Hermitaño added, "Yes, your community and the journey of
Esther resemble one another."

Pedro and the *Hermitaño* saw the *Hermanos* leave the *Morada*
chapel. They then alone pushed their horses down the incline of
the ridge and stopped in by the warm, welcoming sacred adobe.

They dismounted and entered the front door. Hermitaño noticed something he did not recognize in hundreds of years — a skeleton in a wagon in the corner of the front room. He eyes then fixed and gazed upon this remnant and asked, "Is that a dead body with bones with long hair? If that is who I think it is, this has historical significance to the Talmac. I cannot believe this remnant has survived since the beginning of Talmac law!

Doña Sebastiana…La Carreta de muerte-the Cart of Death

That is *Doña Sebastiana. La Carreta de muerte* — the cart of death is the symbol of Doña Sebastiana, used as the hideous skeleton in the cart with a bow and arrow. It was used to symbolize both death and as a symbol of death to the recently recruited or new *Hermano Penitentes* as a fear relic to keep them in order.

To the *Hermandad*, they were not aware that *Doña Sebastiana* served a second and important purpose for the *Ladino Hermanos*. The clean and naked body resembled that of a recently prepared *difunto* — a corpse for a Hebrew burial. The white cloth or sash across the torso is consistent with Jewish law that prescribes burial of a body in plain white shrouds — *tachrichim* so as to demonstrate the equality of all.

The Hermitaño observed her with reverence and said, "The Long Hair of Doña Sebastiana is in accordance with the *Talmud* — the basic book of Jewish law referencing the command from God to Aaron, *that hair for the mourner is not to be trimmed or cut.* The power of death becomes visible to the *Ladino Hermanos* and a reminder of the Hebrew influence upon the Hermandad."

"I get it! I have found you! What tribe do you belong to? The Hermitaño exclaimed.

"We are ourselves; we live at the 33rd Latitude, just as our *pasado*-past in Jerusalem, the Holy City," Pedro explained.

"Tell me of the songs played here by the *Ladino Hermanos*."

"The primary songs were songs of praise called *Alabados*, brought by the original settlers of this territory in 1598. To the Ladinos, the use of Kabbalah techniques to conceal philosophy and survive within Christian *Alabados* was the norm to conceal one's work. These songs originate from the *Petenera* Spanish gypsy genre," Pedro explained.

"Prayer among the *Hermanos* is a group activity rather than an individual practice. *Alabados*, or prayers of praise, are recited and learned as a group. Furthermore, the *Ladino Hermanos* will hold their cryptic Judaic services in the *Morada* on holidays when the Catholic *Hermanos* will be attending the events or holidays that many times are out of the area. The *Alabados* are recited a cappella, in first person, plural form. This style of writing reflects our responsibility for one another and interlinks our fates. The *Alabados* are recited many times after a lighting of candles or the Menorah. The *Ladino*

Hermanos, with the knowledge of the light, share their esoteric wisdom of the cosmos and the Portal of Light with each other. All of this with the ultimate goal to provide a way to create a bond with God by the use of prayer."

Hermitaño asked, "Can you provide me a sample of such a prayer?"

"Yes. The song *Salbe Luna Hermana* — Lord, *Save the Sister Moon* — is a prime example of a Ladino-influenced song of praise. This song has 10 Ladino words among its lyrics, as well as intimate references to their communities of origin. Words from both Basque and Catalán origin will refer to the history of these regions and employs words used only in these areas. The esoteric tone of the *Alabado* alludes to Sun-Light, Sister Moon, Celestial Rays, From the East comes the Sun, and references the writers' knowledge of the Kabbalah.

"*Give glory and great enjoyment in the name of the Mark* (stanza 6), a very unique line in a Christian *Alabado* that refers directly to the *Torah's Joshua 5, Circumcision will be a mark of the covenant between God and Man.*"

Salbe **Luna Hermana**	**Save the Sister Moon**
Dios te *Salbe* Luna Hermana	Lord Save the Sister Moon
Dios te Sol-Luz del dia	Lord of the Sun-Light of the day
Dios te *Salbe* Sol y estuyos	Lord save the Sun and yours.
Los Angeles en el cielo	The angels in the heaven
Los hombres en Alabazos	The men of the psalm prayers
a boca yena digamos	with a full mouth we say
Virgen yena eres de Gracía	Virgin full of Grace
Ruidida atuss santos sus plantas(Rudir-Basquo)	Ascribe to your holy feet
Virgen muerades te pido	Virgin I ask

Consideme las Sertara	Consider for me the Fire
(Sertara-Basquo)	
Pues el Señor es contigo	that the Father is with you
Mas hermosa fue la Luna	More beautiful than the Moon
y mas linda que el Sol eres	and more beautiful than the Sun are you
Desde el perincelpio del mundo	From the beginning of the world
Señora *bendita* le eres	Blessed you are the women
Tan fuera fuestas consifidos	How strongly you were
(Consebir-Esp)	conceived
Sagrada Virgen fiel puedes	Faithful Sacred Virgin
Tenerte por la mejor	You are the best
Entre todas Las Mujeres	of all the Women
Los Angeles en el cielo	The angels of the heaven
Se dan gloria con gran gusto	Give glory with great enjoyment
en el nombre le marca	**in the name of the mark**
De yamos *vendito* el fruto	we bless thy fruit
Del oriente salio el Sol	From the East comes the Sun
Danalo mundo hermosa luz	Give to the world the beautiful Light
De tu boca nacio el *oba*	from your mouth was born the dawn
Y de tu *bientra* Jesús	and from you comes Jesus
Quien dichasa merecierá	Who deserves this happiness
ser tu esclavo madre mis	to be your slave my mother
Con un letrero que el pecho	With your placard upon your breast
Diciendo Santa Maria	To say this is Holy Mary

Dandote el rey celestial	To give to you the celestial rays
	(Portal of Light)
las dones de loes endues	
(Endues-Catalán)	to grant the praise to endure
Eres hija de Dios Padre	You are daughter of Father God
Virgen y Madre de Dios	Virgin and Mother of God
Desde que te coronaron	Since you were crowned
Con diamentes y de flores	with diamonds and flowers
Te supleamos Señora	We supply grand women
Ruegues por los pecados	Prayers for the sins
En fin Divina Señora	In the end divine Woman
Damos tu divina luz	Give us your divine Light
Inbacando ase tu Gracía	We kneel for your Grace
Deciondo asi Amen Jesús	And we say Amen Jesus

*Words in Italics are Ladino (Hebrew-Spanish)

"Was this is shared with the Catholic *Hermanos*?" The Hermitaño asked.

"Not typically. It is used mostly with *Ladino Hermanos*," Pedro answered.

"This is a significant treasure to locate the Mark of the Covenant," the Hermitaño assessed.

"Yes it is," Pedro agreed. "This is why the *Ladino Hermanos* participated in flagellation, the marking of their backs with *la cuerda* — the whip or marking a part of their body. They knew that self-injury was contrary to all Judaic Talmud principles, yet participated in this custom as a remembrance for the harshness of life they endured within the Ladino community."

"Your community possesses an ability to hide in plain sight," the Hermitaño asked. "How have you learned this skill?"

"Concealment is the application of Moshe Cordoviero's PARDES, to conceal your presence in any life situation by means of words, phrase, philosophies and camouflage in any form necessary," Pedro said. "For the Ladino community, to hide has been to endure hardships."

"That was how this story is accepted as genuine, for they have understood the sacrifice it took to survive,"

"You think you can hide an entire play without detection? You have got some tenacity! You are taking great risk that this story will remain within your Ladino families. What are the chances of this working?" Hermitaño asked.

Pedro pondered and looked up to the sky. "There is no limit to the ability of survival," he said. "It is the remnant of faith that kept this community living, and that is why this has worked."

"When in the future will this be shared?" Hermitaño queried.

"At the determination of a turning point in the future, when the values of the people of faith are no longer respected and are repressed. Then a message forward will be sent and the story of this cryptic play will be released," Pedro answered, speaking like a prophet of old.

CHAPTER 5

The Chase

"La Chiva" and **"La Tribunal — Bench"**
2011

Conjunto got up from the table without saying another word. He just left the documents on the glass table as Antonio stared and studied the significance of the two *cuadernos*. As he walked out beneath the Portals, Conjunto wondered, *Did I leave him the sole original cuaderno, or are there more?* He opened Antonio's front door and closed it after he left. *Chin-chin, chin-chin,* his black boots suavely sounded upon the red brick sidewalk straight toward his shiny sky-blue Impala, glistening on the street in front of Washington Park.

As he got in his car, he thought about his next destination, La Chiva. From Antonio's house, he jumped on Louisiana and then turned right on Downing Street. There was a long string of runners and well-paced walkers that ran clockwise around the pathway of the park. *No fat people or fat dogs* in this *barrio* — Latin neighborhood he thought. This park had gorgeous pathways of gray gravel, clean water lakes, sunshine everywhere, and the feeling of good health in abundance. Quite a contrast, to his impoverished cliff reservation life in the arid lands of New Mexico.

Half a mile past the park, he made a left on Speer Boulevard and noticed that the neighborhood began to change. Soon, downtown was in sight as he stopped at a stoplight. A driver to his right in a red sedan pulled up beside him and began staring at his Impala, looking like an undercover cop. The guy noticed the detail of quality workmanship and shininess of Conjunto's car. The red car driver turned his gaze from the car to the driver with his slicked-back black hair and sunglasses. Conjunto's style reminded Antonio of the 1970s band War that played the Low Rider song. When the light turned green, the red car passed Conjunto and his classic Impala.

Conjunto drove beyond downtown and arrived on the north side of Denver to "Chale," the old Latino barrio. *Finally,* he told himself, *maybe I can get some good Mexican food here.*

Conjunto noticed that something had changed since he was there last. Large condominiums had replaced the old houses; sky cranes all over were working on new projects. The north side had transformed into skinny jeans, skinny dogs and dark rimmed glasses. It was now called the Highlands, in reference to the yuppies who had taken over the neighborhood, while the old barrio sat high above the South Platte River on the opposite side of I-25.

What happened to this place? No more brown people, no classic cars — only Toyotas and Subarus; no more fat people and fat dogs, no more dogs barking in the alleys and, most importantly, no more comfortable feel of a Latin barrio that flourished here since the 1940s. He turned right, continued driving on Federal Boulevard. Mexican restaurants were replaced by marijuana shops. The vintage movie house, the Federal Theatre, was now the Victory Church. Maybe next, it will be an office space? The Northside no longer felt like his second home. He continued north to his final destination at 65th and Federal Boulevard.

La Chiva — The goat was known to many as Goat Hill. This barrio was settled by people from New Mexico. The original *Manitos* — persons from New Mexico chose this site for its open spaces around the neighborhood and affordable housing. As he made a right on 65th, he felt the comfort of a barrio with its small, white houses and short wire fences, dogs running loose in the yard, clotheslines for drying clothes and *carne seca* — dry beef. Old vintage American cars on blocks or flat tires were hidden in the long backyards. This was so the *policía* would not notice and give a ticket for an "unmovable car." These cars someday would be rebuilt to their original form and cruised to the north side of Denver, or whatever is left of that barrio. "Hey *ese* — dude, want go for a cruise?"

Manito was a term of endearment among people from New Mexico. The name originated in the mines of Trinidad, Colorado. There, deep in the caves and dark underground, men had to walk distances with head lamps into dark, confined openings that many times required the assistance of another man who offered his hand to move up or down in a tight space. The request, *Dame su mano* — Give me your hand, or *manito*, was a term that remained as a sign of fellowship.

Conjunto parked his car in front of Enselmo's house, an older man in his mid-40s who had lived in this barrio for many decades.

"Conjunto, is that you?" Enselmo called out as he walked out of his house to greet him. "Your car is still 'cherry.' Damn, you take care of that classic! Look at that tight leather, blue interior. Looks like it just came off the factory stock. Makes me feel warm inside."

Conjunto got out of his car and gave Enselmo a big hug — *un abrazo grande*. Hermano Penitentes, even former brothers, never forget one another.

"Gracias, good to see you. I drove through the northside, *pero qué pasó*? What happened to the barrio?"

"The *gringos* finally figured that we were close to downtown and they should move back in. They have been buying everything and scraping, then putting up condo, condo somethings." Enselmo grimaced as he pointed at the pleather buildings. "They call this gentrification — or progress. Never mind what the people who live here think or feel. I do not know where these people get the money to build these plastic buildings."

"Man! Is all of Denver is like this?"

"They are doing this in Five Points, too. The African-American jazz history of Denver will be changed forever. Jazz legends, like

Billie Holiday, Duke Ellington, Dizzy Gillespie, all had family here. They won't be comin' here no mo'. They put a train to go over there. People were already taking buses downtown. They put in an expensive train for what? For who?" Enselmo said with disdain. "But come inside. We need to talk. Bring your bag. You will stay here tonight."

Inside the simple two-bedroom home, a *fogon* — gas heater stood in the corner, and the sofa was covered with a multi-colored braided blanket from parts unknown. A cabinet held knickknacks and medals received by Enselmo's family for service in Vietnam, Korea and WWII.

"*Pareces bien* — you look good," Conjunto said smilingly.

Enselmo was all of 5-foot-6 with brown hair, hazel eyes and a nice smile. He kept in shape with workouts and looked good. Still a working man, he liked the union at his company but was not in love with union management. The ladies thought he was fine with style, and they enjoyed his bravado appearance, being a veteran and all. But aside from his good looks, he was a real American patriot, as was his family. Many think high school is important, but his family had always felt that serving your country in your 20s, with boots on the ground anywhere the president asked, was even more important.

"Still feels like a barrio here," Conjunto said. "It has been a while since I have been here. Tell me, is the *Morada* still down the street?"

The *Morada* was the physical meeting place of the *Hermanos Penitentes*. In this small chapel, the private services were conducted by members. Historically, it was made by the brotherhood from rectangular 12-inch adobe blocks, stacked into walls, three feet wide, and built to hold three rooms.

"It is. Some of my family still attend," Enselmo said.

"*Sientanse* — sit down. Did you meet Antonio?"

"I did. I wish someone would have told me I was dealing with the Sephardim." Conjunto said. "This changes everything, as you know."

The Sephardim translated, literally, to a person of Jewish descent, and originally from Spain. They maintained their Jewish customs with privately practiced Judaic services but, outwardly, practiced Catholic ones. Spanish Catholics called this group "*Marranos*"— swine for this dual practice.

"Yes, this is a unique situation. Did he ask you anything?" Enselmo asked.

"No. But I could tell that he did not understand the request to crack the code," Conjunto said.

"You told him that is was a specific request by the Ladino families?"

"Yes, nothing else."

"Let's get some sleep and talk in the morning, *está bien*?

Morning time here in *La Chiva* still provided a flavor of rural New Mexico. *El gallo* began at sunrise with his cock-a-doodle-doo a few times, as people readied for work. Most people had blue collar jobs — factory workers, maintenance, janitors — dressed in uniforms, and got in their American-made cars to leave for work a little after 7 a.m.

Enselmo's home was what is best described as a sharing home. He shared his home with people who visited. Time was set aside for a good homemade meal, homemade coffee and the beloved tortillas. He awoke early to prepare breakfast and share some quality time with Conjunto before he left.

"*Buenos días*. Did you sleep well? I made *chile rojo con carne*, *frijoles* from the crock pot, *papas, huevos con cebolla* and tortillas for *desayuno* — breakfast.

Do you want café or *jugo* — juice?" Enselmo asked.

"Café, Gracias. You cook better than the reservation. The only thing missing is fry bread," his guest said as he grinned and rubbed his hands together.

Then Conjunto became more serious. "You know, I tossed and turned all night because I could not figure out this Antonio. I was told some things before I left New Mexico, but after meeting him, many things became unresolved in my mind."

"*Pues, vamos a comer* — Well, let's eat. Tell me of your uneasiness," Enselmo said.

"Why would the Ladino families select him to decipher this code?"

"The *cuadernos* you dropped off were in very old Spanish," Enselmo explained. "It was the Spanish that arrived with the original explorers of New Mexico."

"Couldn't they just get an educated professor or someone who understands 16th century Spanish?" Conjunto protested.

"No, I am sure the Ladino families tried that," Enselmo said. "There are two parts to this translation: The first is to translate the Ladino Spanish, and the second is to decipher the codes and clues that deal with the mystical Kabbalah. Really, there are few persons that can do both, and Antonio can be trusted."

"But won't this make him visible, once he shares it?" Conjunto countered.

"To some, he has already been visible; others know nothing." Enselmo said.

"I want to be honest. I was told he could 'see' things that maybe you and I could not! This is why he can decode this much data that comes from very ancient material. Tell me, how can he configure a satellite?" Conjunto pressed his friend, sipping his cáfe.

"I know that he has worked in military secure areas. Maybe he is just a trusted source of information," Enselmo said.

"Those of us from New Mexico know better," Conjunto said "We have dealt with those scientists from Los Alamos. You do not get permission to work on projects without specific skill sets and security clearances. What are his skill sets? You are not telling me anything!" Conjunto lifted his palms upwards to show his uncertainty.

"I know he is a dancer. Enselmos said. "Specialty is Latin dance. Danced in Puerto Rico, Miami, the Caribbean. In Europe he has danced in Spain, France, Italy, and Germany, all over the world. He is also a singer. His genre is gypsy Flamenco, *Cante Jondo*, which originated in southern Spain. Here, he sings our *Alabados*."

"What does that have to do with a satellite?" Conjunto was becoming more frustrated.

"The Kabbalah, and the skill to be able to conceal himself."

"Enselmo, I was born at night, but not last night. Satellites and Flamenco gypsy music are polar opposites." Conjunto looked sternly at his friend for avoiding his questions.

"Are they? The Sephardim-Seraditas hid their lyrics in the *Alabados*, which were previously borrowed from the flamenco music called the Petanera." Enselmo lowered his voice. "The Sephardim-Seraditas hid their knowledge of the cosmos in the play that you delivered to Antonio, and he will decipher this play. The skill set to work on a satellite is a function of this spatial intelligence. The ability to exist, hiding in plain sight, is an esoteric skill of the Sephardic Jews. It is a higher level ability, yet they are the same skill. Do you see how Antonio is able to function at a seemingly invisible level? This is hard to understand because it is an esoteric level of living, yet that's how it works."

Conjunto shook his head, trying to grasp this concept. "The frontal part of my brain just woke up. Living at an invisible level provides the ability to perform at a higher level. Where is this learned from?"

"Seraditas have been doing this since the 13th century in Spain. Prior to this, maybe the Sinai Mountains," Enselmo replied, then looked keenly at Conjunto. "Antonio does not know me and will never know me. He knows you and will figure out who you are and will want to know why you were chosen. He is very sharp; he has glanced at your license plate, and he will quickly determine who you are."

"There is something important you need to know," Conjunto divulged. In his home I saw ... I saw ... He has *"La Tribunal* — the Bench!

Enselmo was immediately taken aback. Pausing, his lips slowly opened, his hand trembled and reached to the front of his forehead. After a long pause he muttered, "Wonder who gave him *La Tribunal?"*

The *Cuadernos* were Shared with the Chairwoman
Denver, Colorado
Fall 2011

Upon graduating from Amherst College and arriving in Denver in the early 1970s, the Chairwomen Maddox rented an apartment in Northwest Denver. Excited about learning and living in the Mile High City, she still wanted to maintain her connection to her roots. She looked in the phone book to locate the nearest Catholic church and found the historic St. Catherines at 42nd and Federal Boulevard. From then on she attended church regularly alone. She caught the eye of and befriended Father Martin, then an aged Dominican trained priest.

At 18, Father Martin had served as a young medic in the WWII Medical Services unit, where he cared for many wounded. It was there that he also saw how the chaplains comforted the dying and heard their confessions before blessing them for the last time. He was inspired by the brave young men and women who unselfishly gave of themselves to serve their country, but he was equally inspired by the priests who devoted their lives to serving the soldiers in their darkest hours.

Upon returning to the homeland, he entered the seminary in Denver and was later assigned to serve the multicultural German, Italian and Mexican neighborhoods in Northwest Denver. As a priest, he said Mass and heard confessions at dawn and dusk, a tradition he still continued at this church in remembrance of those who gave of themselves in the armed services. He always knew he would hear the heartbeat of the community by working alongside those who had served in the military.

One early snowy morning, Father Martin was sitting alone in St. Catherine's Church, in his morning meditation, when a Hispanic elderly woman he had long known in the parish came in and knelt behind him. After a few minutes offering her own prayers, she looked around to make sure no one else had entered the church before tapping Father Martin on the shoulder. She told him that she had something important to tell him and did he have time to listen. He nodded his head that he did, so she then started to tell him the story of the mysterious *cuadernos*.

He was aware of the Judaic background of people from Southern Colorado and Northern New Mexico, from among his family of priests. He also knew that the depth of faith from this community was neither explainable nor comparable. The elderly woman's profound knowledge of the *cuadernos* led him to believe in the actual merit of the cryptic message found in the *cuadernos*.

Chairwoman Maddox was a true-blue Democrat. Brought up in a blue-collar town in western Pennsylvania, her father was a deep cavern coal miner, and her mother was a teacher. As a young adult, she fought for real women's issues and civil rights in the late 1960s, burned her bra, hid draft dodgers, marched with the Poor People's Campaign in the South, and was ready to take on the world.

As an integral part of the Democratic National Committee (DNC) and a carpetbagger, she ran for political office and won with the fortitude and work ethic she had learned from her parents. She rose up the ladder and became the head of the national DNC. As with almost all politicians, she listened to financial donors and their big money to benefit her career and the progressive liberal politics that influence party politics. More importantly, she had learned to adeptly use the rights of small people to align with the individual needs of big donors whose values did not represent those of the faithful. The small people, who are the faithful people, the less educated, less wealthy, still believed the Democratic Party was the main focus of their issues.

Father Martin knew that the chairwoman was a major player in the Democratic National Party and asked her to coffee and shared the story of the *cuadernos* with her. The priest knew the chairwomen was not connecting to the spirituality of the church, but from what she had told him about her father's background, he felt that the story of the cryptic Judaic faith might lead her to better understand the fabric of her father's spirituality. The priest shared with her that *cuadernos* connected to the original Creation and of the existence of Antonio. Why he chose a Sacrament Catholic to share this story is a mystery, yet he shared with her the genuine faith that her father possessed and somehow thought it would benefit her faith.

Father Martin was not cognizant of how much she had changed to become a progressive liberal from her early days in Denver. At the same time, the old war horse priest actually did understand that, at the bottom of her heart, in the *mero mero* — midde of her soul, the mystery of the Messiah resided.

It was with foreknowledge given to her by the priest about the *cuadernos* that the chairwoman began her research on Antonio, only to find much more than a mysterious story that was to be revealed in her backyard. She said to herself, *to know the Messiah, my father was tested, challenged, but he knew the Messiah. This is something I do not understand. Can these cuadernos show me the Messiah?*

La Matanza
Near Chupadero, NM
Fall 2010

In the early fall of 2010, the Ladino families summoned Antonio to meet in the small town of Chupadero, an hour north of Santa Fe, New Mexico. They asked him to meet, not in a building or a home, but at a crossroads near a meadow where the grass and alfalfa wheat were still low-cut from the fall harvest.

Antonio arrived at this crossroads at midday. A man flagged him down to stop in the vicinity of the parked cars lined up on both sides of the county road. He heard a buzz, an excitement from the many people gathered far away, and he wondered what all the excitement was about.

He saw the small group of men and women gathered away from the excitement, intently looking on from afar. Antonio walked up to this group and asked, "Did you summon me?"

A man who did not provide his name asked in return, "Are you Antonio from Denver?" as he noticed the green Colorado license plate. "We have been awaiting you. We want you to look at all the people gathered here."

From a distance, one could see men, boys and young girls lined across a central position. The man in the center held an animal, which appeared to be a young pig squirming and snorting to get out of the man's grasp. The man knelt down, the shimmering skin of the glossy, greased pig sparkled in the sun, and the pig began to jump out of the man's hands. All at once, the pig hit the ground running and snorting, going into the empty grass field. The line of people set out to pursue the pig with grand smiles and laughter as they ran and dove in vain to grab this greased animal.

Antonio looked over at the small group of people standing away from the excitement who met him. The dull look in their eyes and fearful straight faces showed not one glimmer of hope from this concerned group. Antonio understood the silence, as a second young greased pig was released in the meadow. Young and old alike pursued and grabbed at the pig until it was captured. The beast was then taken to slaughter to reenact the Judaic slaughter by the Inquisition and the Alhambra decree of 1492. The beast was struck by a blow from a blunt ax head just above the two eyes on the forehead to knock him unconscious. They sliced his neck and hung his body up to drain the blood into large pans for seven days. The blood was strained and fried with onions, salt and *quelite* — wild spinach as a tasty winter meal.

They roasted the pig and shared it with the community, including the Ladino families that participated in this pastime to preserve their true identities. The Ladino people who participated in this charade were required to eat the flesh of this beast. *Blessed be those who eat of this flesh and know the mosaic law of Moses*, Antonio said to himself, for he knew they participated in this ritual to survive.

In an unusual twist, in keeping with Jewish customs (*Costumbres de los Judios*), the meat of the first beast was not eaten for seven days after slaughter by the Christians. Only organs such as the heart or the liver were eaten immediately.

This reenactment had been ongoing for hundreds of years. It did not bring smiles or pleasure to everyone. As the small group began to break up, an anonymous man said to Antonio, "We will be in contact with you soon."

Chase Scene and Demos
Fall 2012
Denver Colorado

The reading of the English version of the original play occurred in December 2012 at the Common Grounds coffee shop in northwest

Denver to coincide with the beginning of the astrological age of Aquarius. A small group of readers took the roles of various characters and completed the reading of the ancient play. Enselmo had been apprised of the reading and had asked Conjunto to stop by and be a witness to a momentous divulgence.

During the reading, Antonio noticed two men of suspicious nature sitting at a table, watching from afar. At the end of reading, the two men approached Antonio and looked down at the table at the *cuadernos* and reached for the notebooks. Antonio anticipated this move and quickly grabbed the *cuadernos*, throwing the old brown chair behind him on the floor to make a move to run out the back door. As he fled outside, to his surprise, Conjunto was waiting in his souped-up 1966 sky-blue Impala.

Instinctively, Antonio jumped in. "*Agrenias — vamanos —* Hurry — let's go," he told the driver as he turned his head and saw the two perps heading to their car. The Impala peeled out on Lowell Boulevard and 32nd, heading north to Rocky Mountain Lake Park. Still, Antonio was curious. "Why are you here, still in Denver? We've got to lose these guys."

"You are lucky, man, that I came back to hear this reading. Who are those vatos, anyway?" Conjunto asked.

"They're driving a Subaru?" Antonio said as the two men jumped into the car. "Could it not be any more obvious? They got no style."

"*Quienes son? —* Who are they?" Conjunto asked.

"Those are wise guys from Demos."

"Who is Demos?" Conjunto asked.

"Demos is an organization that uses fronts to conceal and achieve nasty lifestyles. Civil rights for individual needs, teachers and their unions convert minds of children from traditional families to liberal causes, the list goes on." Antonio looked back and soothed down as they made distance from their pursuers.

Conjunto was now in third gear, with the Subaru still in chase. He asked, "Where do I go?"

"Make a right here — hard!" Antonio ordered as the Impala's back end swung up and turned into Carl's Pizzeria.

Conjunto turned off the lights and the Subaru sped by, following nothing.

Antonio sighed with relief. "Saved my *nalga* — backside. I did not expect to see you. What brought you to the reading? I saw you drinking coffee earlier."

"I just came to visit an artist friend, a Chicana. She was one of the readers of the play. And the play is read in December 2012," Conjunto said.

"Yes, the play has been translated and read as a play in its original form," Antonio explained as he raised his fists in victory.

"Just as requested by the Ladino families," Conjunto observed. "Why is this so critical?"

"Tell me, Conjunto, you came back to Denver, and you located the play being read. What do you know about all of this?" Antonio asked as the aroma of the delicious pizza consumed the night air and filled the moonstruck blue low rider.

"I knew this *cuaderno* has importance beyond a simple translation. The heads of the Ladino families and the elders in my tribe sent me with the *cuadernos* to you, to be deciphered. Now I see the play has been has been read in 2012. Two wise guys are after the *cuadernos* and you. I came to figure out why this puzzle is so important."

"Let's get a slice of pizza," Antonio said and opened the car door. "I'm really grateful you were outside waiting for me."

Carl's Pizzeria was a Denver landmark since 1950. As the men walked into the double-entry doorway, the 1960s leather booths with gray tables greeted them. The burgundy walls were accented with silver frame prints of Frank Sinatra, Dean Martin and Tony Bennett. The aroma of Italian sauces and pizza filled every sense of their nostrils. Splattered spaghetti sauce remained on bench backs, the mark of a real Italian eatery. The music from the original jukebox played the soulful sounds from the Platters' "Smoke Gets in your Eyes" and Smokey Robinson's "Shop Around" to the early tunes of Marvin Gaye.

Antonio motioned to the jukebox. "It's America at its finest." It's almost a forgotten memory of life gone by. Not much can make you feel better than this pizza that is about to be ordered.

Conjunto nodded in agreement as the men sat in the dark tan booth, unnoticed way back of the restaurant. "Man, this place is another era, another time."

"Now you got it. That is what this play is. A story from another time frame, now coming forward to this time," Antonio explained.

The waitress, dressed in a "penny," a one-piece pink uniform with a green apron, took their order — a large pepperoni with green chile slices as the topping and *chile pequí* as a side topping, also known as red-hot flakes. She brought out two tall, ice-cold Cokes served in red plastic cups before the pizza. Then came the steaming hot pizza, just as they had ordered. This is the way New Mexicans eat; this way they can go anywhere and never get an upset stomach.

"How does this come forward? I mean why is my tribe involved?" Conjunto asked.

"Your Acoma cliff dwellers came from the ancient Anasazi tribe. You are timekeepers. You preserve time, and you preserved this story in this *cuaderno*." Just then, something caught Antonio's eye as he looked out the side window and noticed the Subaru driving along the front side of the restaurant. "We gotta go," he said abruptly as he laid a $20 bill on the table. The two men slid low from their booth, then skipped out the back door and rushed into the Impala. "Back out quietly and take me to my truck," he told Conjunto.

They quietly drove back to the coffee shop and stopped by Antonio's silver Chevy Silverado. "Pretty sweet *troca* — truck," Conjunto offered his praise. "I need to know more. When can we meet?"

"Maybe I will contact you," Antonio said as he jumped out of the classic American two- door and headed toward his truck.

Conjunto drove off to stay with Enselmo, churning over the night's events in his mind. *I wonder who are the Demos, and why do they want to stop the sharing of the cuaderno?*

Subaru Guys and the Chairwomen
Fall 2012
Downtown Denver, Colorado

The Subaru Guys returned to the headquarters of the Democratic National Party. The brain trust had selected a low-rent neighborhood location away from the downtown area to provide the appearance of "We are the people." The real decision makers all had swanky downtown offices with thick mahogany office furniture and fancy boardrooms, similar to their Republican counterparts, a complement to the almost oneness of both political philosophies.

The Chairwoman asked, "Did you get the *cuadernos?*"

"We tried, but Antonio picked them up when he saw us, and then he and this other guy fled out the back door to an awaiting Impala. We pursued them in my car, but they took off to the north side of Denver and we eventually lost them," Subaru Todger explained lamely.

"The *cuadernos* — they have not been published yet. We need to suppress them so they will not be made available to be presented to the public again. Damn it!" the Chairwoman said as she slammed her palm against the mahogany desk.

"What are these *cuadernos?* What could they possibly do?"

"My concern is that the influence of these *cuadernos* may awaken a sleeping giant — the faithful, the Christians, and give them the backbone to question the Democrats' policies," she explained.

"What can we do? We don't need that."

"You, you and your boyfriend here, Champion. Don't look surprised. I do my homework." The Subaru guys looked at each other. "Give me details on who these two men are."

"I heard the *cuadernos* are being written as a novel; find out when it is to be completed, who the editors and publishers are. We have many allies in the liberal media. We need to make them aware that they do not share, publish, or use these writings at their colleges, high schools or media outlets. We need to spin this as work from just some common folk who created an unbelievable story."

Subaru Todger, surprised to be recognized as half of a couple, said, "We can place pressure on this Antonio, make sure he knows no one is going to buy this story. Make sure nothing came out of these *cuadernos*."

"These *cuadernos* are very old; they are a link to the very first Europeans that arrived in our American Southwest. The message and knowledge of the *cuadernos* could challenge the Democratic Party's existence. The working faithful can demonstrate we no longer provide policy for the working class, but rather for individual needs, like your lifestyle. Do not be in contact with this Antonio until I tell you to," the Chairwoman demanded.

"I don't understand. We could have located him and these *cuadernos* to make sure nothing is revealed," Subaru Todger said forcefully.

"Go and get me my research on these two men. That's what I want you to do," she said bluntly as the Subaru Guys left the office.

The Chairwoman knew she had entered a spiritual battle that would not vanish or cease. It was a battle from the creation of man, a battle in which she knew she would be unable to see her foe, a battle that would attack her and her party on a conscious and subconscious level. She knew she had crossed a line, a line crossed that suppressed Creation. And all this to advance her career and entitle a few with select individual needs.

What kept coming into her mind was her father, who worked to his death with faith in his Messiah. But it was a faith she could never come to grips with to understand his courage and why he kept going back to the mines. Now she wondered, *Have I become the dust in the mines?*

Conjunto and the Acoma Tribe
Fall 2012

Conjunto left Antonio at his truck and departed briskly from the coffee shop after the chase. He knew he had encountered the Sephardim and had seen the bench at Antonio's home. This unsettled both his mind and soul. His medicine man grandfather had shared with him the organic mystical capability of the Sephardim. They call themselves Ladino, for their ability to speak the hybrid tongue of Spanish and Hebrew. Yet there was a longstanding relationship established between Native Americans and the Spanish Jews; they are known as the Sephardim-*Sefarditas*.

As Conjunto drove away from Antonio's home, he had left a clue in the form of the sun. The New Mexico license place is depicted with the sun yellow Zia Sun symbol to the left of center and USA imprint, centered at the bottom. These symbols were to make the rest of the country realize that New Mexico was part of the USA. In the middle of the plate is the seal of Acoma nation.

Not too many decked-out 1966 sky-blue Impalas in the Acoma nation. This will be an easy trace, Antonio said to himself as he drove off in his truck. He began the thought process to figure out this delivery man. *Yet, why did they choose him to deliver the cuadernos?*

Antonio began researching the Acoma Pueblo and soon realized that there was a strong Christian presence among the Acoma, so there could be a longstanding relationship between the Hermandad and this tribe.

The Acoma tribe, in its long history, was almost invincible. It had never lost a single battle to other native tribes, due to the fact that their strategic cliff fortress made their land almost unconquerable. However, in 1599 in the Battle of Acoma Pueblo, the Spanish scaled the cliffs and triumphed over the defending tribesmen. Going up against a repressed Sephardim is not good luck for any foe. It has been that way and will always be that way. Subsequent events of cruelty by the Spanish created a negative view of them, yet the Catholic faith was shared within the cliff homes and Christianity has been practiced there ever since.

The Acoma tribe descended from the Anasazi people of Chaco Canyon in northwestern New Mexico. The Anasazi people were a direct lineage to the Aztecs and built their cliff dwellings in perfect north-south alignment with the capital city of Tenochtitlan. The Anasazi studied the sun, and this knowledge passed on to the medicine men elders of Acoma cliff villages.

The *Ladino Hermanos de Luz* — Brothers of Light and the Acoma medicine men shared three important commonalities. They were both repressed by the Spanish Catholic Church, and both had knowledge of the cosmos through the study of the movement of the sun. They also believed in Christ and his faith, even though they did not feel comfortable at times sharing this with other Christians.

Since Antonio had a keen eye for the possible locations of where the *Moradas* resided, this would be his key to locating *Ladino Hermanos*. He pulled out his New Mexico map. *I thought so. Grants — This is where the silver mines existed.*

This is where a vast number of Moradas sprang up, always following the work, Antonio said to himself. Grants Mines were less than a 30-minute drive from Acoma Pueblo. This is where both the Native Americans and the Spanish worked and got to know one another.

He realized that there was a strong Christian presence and there could be an established relationship between the Hermandad and this tribe.

Fear and faith accompany one another, and both groups found solace in the profound words of the *Alabados*. The mines are dark and dangerous, where injury or death can arrive at any second. Faith is the only way that miners get through their dangerous, unpredictable day.

Antonio said to himself, *The Ladino families would not share the Portal of Light detail with Conjunto, but they would ask him to drive the documents to me to conceal their identities. He may know of the Sephardim; there is a long standing relationship between the Acomas and the Sephardims. Was it likely that the Ladino families hid the cuadernos within the Acoma tribe for that reason?*

Conjunto's Native American family did practice the Catholic religion. Some that worked outside of the cliff homes even became *Hermanos* Penitentes. It is with this history that Conjunto was chosen to deliver the *cuadernos*, Antonio's research revealed.

Conjunto likely knows of the movement patterns of the sun. The *Hermanos de Luz* — Brothers of Light would be interested in their tribe's knowledge, Antonio surmised. The Catholics generally disregarded sun patterns as worthless, yet the *Ladino Hermanos* know that the symbol of the sun is of great value.

I now see why Conjunto was given an important task. His tribe has earned this privilege. Their counsel may have affirmed the presence of the 'First Sun'. This to be shared with the Acoma elders, Antonio thought to himself.

CHAPTER 6
The Moral Dilemma

The Chairwoman

While most of the major rights of equality, welfare, poverty and healthcare had all passed in decades past, rights known as the individual nasty rights have quietly been masked as small people's rights, but really have nothing to do with the working class. Amazingly, slogans such as "National Healthcare for All" and "It Takes a Village to raise a Child" are a facade, for the real work is done behind the scene to pass specific individual rights of those money-funders.

The chairwoman was aware that this facade was growing thin, and in her position as a top level "politica," looking down on her constituency, she knew something or someone could wake up the sleeping faithful and catch on to the fact that the Democratic Party created laws for those with money. Her party recently passed the major American Healthcare Reform Act and found itself acquiescing to large healthcare carriers to provide Americans the large (as in $10,000-$25,000) deductibles in catastrophic plans and having the audacity to call this a health plan for families.

Throughout this lengthy liberal political life she had lived, she had maintained her faith and had continued to attend church regularly. She is what is called a Sacrament Catholic, one who believed in Baptism, Eucharist, Confirmation and Holy Orders, but will not support or vote for her church's social issues on abortion, contraceptives, divorce, homosexuality, LBGT rights, synthetic children and body parts or the sole use of male priests.

She had always felt unsettled, for her political views were contrary to those of her church, yet on a deeper level, her faith and her father had told her that her politics do not reflect that of the working poor — the faithful — and this bothered her immensely. Yet she knew that her workday adhered to the individual needs of the moneyed people and not to the working poor or faithful of her party. Spending her day providing advancement and opportunity for those with immoral lifestyles — who were never poor — never faithful, and privy to the wealthy constituents who would keep her safely in her lofty position, was now her sole purpose. Simply, she learned to look the other way and forgot the genuine, oppressed people who got her to this position in the first place. Yet she never had forgotten that she had witnessed real faith, seeing her father kneeling at the cross and thanking the Lord for bringing him home to his family and for giving him the strength the next day to return to the dust of the mines.

In the back of her mind, her conscience always told her that an issue of faith would force her to reveal her party's true motivation. Her party had changed, and now the powerful individual — needs resources far outweighed the needs of the working class. Now, whatever loopholes that could advance these individual needs would far outweigh the original intention of any laws that were passed.

Finally, a faith issue was challenging her politics in the form of a story of the faithful poor that would bring something she knew she was not equipped to handle — the Messiah. Had she gone so far and repressed the real poor to the point that a repressed people would align the Messiah against her politics? This, she was beginning to fear. Had she and her party's politics become the pharaoh of Egypt, the slave masters of the American South? And, now, were the bearers of repression crying out for freedom? The more she pondered these questions, the more panic-stricken she became because she knew, in her heart, that the Lord heard the cries of the faithful repressed.

Demos and the Chairwoman
Downtown Denver, Colorado
Fall 2012

2012 was an election year, and in November the Democratic Party members were celebrating the re-election of their candidates at the downtown Denver Marriott. The Colorado Democratic Party had changed a lot over time; its elected officials were now mostly all from out of state. They listened and voted based on money; it didn't matter what you looked like or who you slept with. You did not see families or the virtue of family values attending their gatherings any more. The politicos used terms phrases like "caring for children" and "college assistance plans" when, in reality, they supported teachers and their unions, and non-conventional families, whose values are diametrically opposite the values of the traditional families from which the students originated.

Antonio planned to attend the Democratic election party at the Denver Marriott that November night because he knew the Subaru henchmen would likely be there, along with the honchos that sent them. *Always best to surprise your foe in their nose hairs,* Antonio reminded himself. Then he decided to call Conjunto and invite him to come with him.

"Dime, this is Conjunto," his friend answered his cell.

"Conjunto, this is Antonio." I have been thinking. Would you like to meet this evening? We can talk. But first we will visit those Subaru guys. What do you think?"

"I am down for it. I did not like being chased. Not the Indian Way."

"This will take your Native American Skin bravery. Dress in a suit coat. We will be going to a nice place. But first, meet me at St. Catherine's Church, 26th and Federal at 7:00. They are open late," Antonio explained, "They have had both Masses and Confessions at the early 6 a.m. and at the late-evening service every week day since World War II in remembrance of those who have served and fallen."

Antonio arrived early at St. Catherine's, a church built with the traditional architecture of large doorways and columns that gave it the look of so many old European churches. The interior resonated with the calm, cool air from the high cathedral ceilings, and an ambiance of solemn grace filled the church. Dressed in a dark sport coat, a light shirt with a sharp collar and tan boots from Clark Shoes, Antonio would fit in at the Democrats' Celebration Extravaganza.

Conjunto arrived a few minutes late, cool and nonchalant, like the other side of the pillow on a very hot night, dressed like *un vato verdadero* — a true cool character in a tan, short-sleeve guavabera shirt with front pockets, tan pants that cuff just above the skinny black boots with taps that *chin-chin*, as he walked in. His slick, dark black hair was pulled back with barber gel to give that sheen to only the most *chebere* — cool!

Conjunto saw Antonio sitting in the calm of the church, one quarter way down the aisle, so he walked gingerly to avoid the *chin-chin* as he sat next to Antonio.

"*Aquí llegué* — I finally made it here. This is the only place where the calm of the Earth still resonates. Let me take a moment to center this calm in my soul," Conjunto almost whispered as he slowly relaxed. "Before we go anywhere, *quiero decirme de este cuenta* — tell me of this story." Antonio looked at Conjunto's attire and thought to himself, *He has the faith I need and the balls to fight for the spirit of the Lord.*

Antonio agreed to tell him about the *cuaderno*. "The story in is two parts. First, it is an alternate view of the birth of the Emmanuel, and secondly, the deciphered play is the cryptic story of the Jewish history from the peoples of New Mexico and Southern Colorado. Lastly, the story calls for the Messiah to appear."

"And the Demos? Are they afraid of the arrival of the Messiah?" Conjunto asked.

"Yes, they fear that the real Christians will be awakened and question their motives for the laws and antifamily values they support when they are supposed to be protectors of the workers and their families," Antonio explained.

"If they do that, the Messiah will put the *hurt* on these people."

"Yes, they know this will happen if this story is shared," Antonio agreed. "But I want to surprise them by arriving at their celebration party tonight. They know I am a Special Government Agent, but they will be uncertain if they should be tracked by my agency, once they have been identified. It will become a chess match. If we do this properly, they will not know how to react to us. Can we take your car? I like to drive in style."

When Conjunto and Antonio jumped into the Impala, Conjunto pushed a cassette tape into the vintage silver-and-black player, and the tune of "*Las nubes que van pasando se paran*" sounded over the stock speakers with the original crackling background.

"Mr. Brown Soul himself," Antonio said out loud.

"You got it man. Little Joe y la Familia. *A dónde vamos?*" Conjunto asked.

"To the Marriot Hotel downtown. We're going to a party that's going to rumble!"

The perfect humming of the original engine gave pause to know that American workmanship can still perform splendidly 50 years later.

"Where should we park?" Conjunto asked.

"At this place, find the lot with a bunch of Subarus," Antonio said laughingly.

They arrived at the hotel and, luckily, located a parking space close to the front doors.

Antonio thought, *These people have become the Democratic Party of One's Needs. Wonder if they ever see what they have become?*

Conjunto and Antonio went through the large double-glass doors and took the elevator to the third floor where the giant ballroom was located. They entered the room and looked around. Not a child or family in sight. Antonio thought, *If this is a workers' party, dress suits must be the attire for hospital staff and the janitorial union.* The two men clung close to the walls as they walked around the room, two sets of eyes checking out all the people.

Something odd caught the eye of Conjunto as he nodded his head toward the an impressive chamber separated for members of the LBGT community, a room filled with women dress in men's style suites and short haircuts of men. Conjunto said to Antonio, "Is that the place for the origin of the synthetic children?"

"Now you are getting it." Antonio answered

Conjunto stopped and nodded his head forward. "Over there, near the stage. Do you see the Subaru guys dressed in suits?"

Antonio recognized them, and this interested him, for they were taking directives from none other than Marybeth Maddox, the Chairwoman of Democratic National Committee. She was a former Colorado state senator, a sham Christian who attended Mass regularly and had been a party leader for decades.

Dressed in strict business attire of a dark-tan fitting coat with a tight beige skirt, with see-through tan stockings and dark shoes, she looked like she had lost her soul to power and money decades prior.

Antonio and Conjunto calmly walked toward the group and stopped a few feet away, catching the attention of both Subaru guys. Their eyes widened and glared, as they did not know how to react. The Chairwoman's eyes blinked, her head bobbled, her face grew gray and her mouth drew open. She knew she had been identified as the honcho who sent the Suburu guys to steal the *cuadernos.*

Antonio looked directly at madam chairwoman and said, "The story has been deciphered, and the play has been read in public. You and your wise guys have been identified. Your move is next, or should it be mine?"

Conjunto stared fearlessly at the Subaru guys and said, "You, *ese,* you're next!" as he nodded towards the men.

Conjunto and Antonio stepped back slowly and melted into the crowd. They walked out the hall and took the elevator, with no one in pursuit. Finally outside the building, they hurried into the Impala.

"*Tú los espantaste* — You sure scared *them!*" Conjunto said as the car started on a dime and they purred away, ever so slowly in the Impala, shining in the moonlight.

"Did you see their faces? They looked like their retirement plan was just taken away! And she has *cara* — face to call herself 'Mary!' "What a sham!" Conjunto said as he shook his head no-o-o and his face grinned with disbelief. He then turned the black leather oval steering wheel to guide the natural bounce of the Impala as they peeled away from downtown.

"Vamos! They may be following. *Llévame a mi troca* — Take me to my truck" Antonio said, as he looked behind to see that they were not being followed.

"Antonio, I now understand why you were selected to decipher the play," Conjunto said, stopping the Impala in front of his friend's truck.

"Talk to you soon," Antonio said as he got out of the Impala and walked into the night.

Basilica and the Confession Booth
Christmas Eve, 2012

Midnight Mass for Christmas Eve at the Cathedral Basilica of the Immaculate Conception is a very special day for Catholics, and on this late evening the archbishop delivered the Mass to a packed house with standing room only. The cathedral was decked out with holiday colors of green and red ribbon bows along the altar and extra candles were lit for a High Mass. The archbishop wore the tall mitre hat with cuffs along the side to signify his distinguished level of importance. His hat was reminiscent of *the* tall hat worn by the Grand Poobah in the Moose Lodge in the cartoon series the *Flintstones*. During the Scripture readings, he sat at the *Kathedra* chair, a white, marble seat with spires that shot up the back side to match the design of the church's interior.

The Gothic vaulted ceilings were held up by trinity rib columns made of marble, soaring hundreds of feet into the air. Bell spires, reaching high toward the ceiling, were made of white granite and marble, which match the altar and pulpit, carved from Italian Carrara marble. The half-oval, stained-glass windows depicted Bible stories with figures of Jesus, Mother Mary, and the Disciples, all with the distinctive halo-esque aura glowing over their heads.

The birch-wood confessional booth, where the priests heard the guilt of sinners, was located in the back of the church, and on this special evening, a long line of wrongdoers stood in line to confess their soul's. As Antonio looked at the imposing figures surrounding the altar, he thought, *These priests have not seen real contrition for sins, like for those sins confessed as the Ladino Hermanos bore heart and soul, tears and sweat, cries and moans, to the Higher Being God on the Tribunal-Bench within the Moradas.*

In the background for the Communion ritual that night, the choir was singing Ave Verum Corpus to Jesus, Son of God, sung in the historical Latin lyrics and accompanied by the imposing pipe organ. As Antonio was returning from receiving Communion, he was touched by the ancient lyrics that sounded so much like Spanish. He was walking toward the back of the church toward his seat when he crossed in front of the outer doors of the confessional booth and was startled to notice the Chairwoman stepping out from the booth. At that instant, he couldn't help himself from boldly approaching her.

"Did you relieve your conscience, or just tell the priest the sins you think are veniable-forgivable? I bet most of your sins were legislative or administrative, but you have not a clue!" His head and shoulders weaved in unison on each vowel.

The Chairwoman was just as shocked to see Antonio. "Funny, I didn't think special agents attended Mass. Who knows what type of things *you've* done. Maybe the priests don't have the conscience to hear what *you've* done." As she and Antonio naturally sauntered into a quiet corner of the Basilica, a standoff was about to begin. "By the way, are you even Catholic?" she whispered with disdain. "Or just in public? You know, I hear you swing both ways. Are you with the Cross or with Moses?"

"You might learn something by studying the works of the Torah. Ever hear of the Old Testament? But you could start by being a real Christian," Antonio countered.

"What about you? So pious, so angelic! Who knows what your agency does with the information you so adeptly collect? All of the world thinks you are just an insurance agent," the Chairwoman skillfully pointed out.

"You and your party have crossed the line of Creation. Your policies are repressive to the organic creation of life by the Higher Being God. You have exploited the workers, the faithful, and aligned yourself with large corporations and their immoral policies. Money must be pretty good to use the civil rights of the oppressed for the rights of the nasty."

The Chairwoman just glared at Antonio,

"Tell me, did you tell of your real sins in the confessional booth? Providing protection for homosexuality, abortion, birth control, synthetic body parts and children, all at the expense of the workers?" Antonio drilled in.

The Chairwoman's eyes looked down, feeling shame in this tender Christmas Eve moment. She knew her party provided rights to those disdained by the church. She also knew Antonio was right; the poor and faithful had been used to provide individual rights for wealthy supporters, yet she would not concede this, for it was her lifetime of work.

"Times have changed; policies and priorities have changed. Get with the program! Nothing can stop this liberal process now," the chairwoman said clenching her teeth.

"That is why the story of the *cuaderno* has been deciphered. The repressed Judaic community had the inalienable right to call for the coming of the Messiah from the Higher Being God," Antonio stated firmly.

At these words, the Chairwoman trembled inside, and her hands began to shiver. "Sure of this, are you?" She demanded, trying to sound strong, yet fear had gripped her soul. Though her Scottish-German blood began to curl in her veins, she knew the Messiah would listen to the pleas of the faithful repressed.

"This is how Jesus of Nazareth appeared; he was asked to provide liberty from oppression among the Judaic faithful when they asked for a Messiah," Antonio explained. "It is now such openly gay times of repression on our faith that it is almost an open joke upon the faithful."

The Chairwoman froze and looked at Antonio with caution. She confoundedly asked, "What does this have to do with your *cuaderno*?"

"The cryptic play is summoning the Messiah. Your party's policies are permitting repression upon the faithful, and the pleas are being listened to by the Higher Being God," Antonio explained.

"The sacred Judaic history of characters, symbols, prayers and latitude markers are ingrained in the original formation of both the *Hermanos Penitentes* and the *Morada*. As the *cuadernos* arrived to the now of today, the non-disclosed cryptic concepts are a continued legacy, even though the practices of the Inquisition no longer have an exterior presence," Antonio explained further.

Never in her mind did the Chairwoman think that her life's work, her party's policies, would cause repression and for the pleas of the Messiah to arrive. She then asked, "Where does this story originate?"

"The same locale as the first Jewish Christians who protected the newborn baby Jesus of Nazareth, the Judaic shepherd families from the Sinai Mountains," Antonio explained.

The Chairwoman was profoundly bewildered and humbled. She had forgotten why the Emmanuel had arrived in the first place, to provide liberation to those repressed. She then remembered her father, her only witness to real faith that she had ever encountered, kneeling and bowing to the crucifix. She now realized he was not seeking the strength to return to the coal mines; rather, he was requesting liberation from the life of the coal mines and praying for the Messiah to lead him from servitude.

As the solemn and tender emotion of that first Christmas night seeped into her soul, she realized that her life's work, which had begun in helping the underserved women and persons of color, had evolved into providing rights for those whose lifestyle of choice is protected at the expense of the poor and faithful.

"The faithful people of color have never received the advantages of civil rights benefits into the corporate and private sectors. The uniqueness that the Ladino community has seen and felt the additional repression of Creation by the passage of laws of abortion, birth control, LGBT rights, synthetic children and adults ensured that the natural rights of the human will continue to be disrespected and no longer valued," Antonio explained.

"Why is this happening now?" The Chairwoman asked.

"This year, the year of 2012, is the beginning year of the Age of Aquarius, the age of Women in the Constellations. This upcoming age and the repression of Creation is a singular collision of events," Antonio explained quietly in the corner of the Basilica.

The Chairwoman looked at the face of Antonio, then deeply into his eyes. She saw the real faith, the faith that did not possess fear, the faith that kept the covenants of the Lord. This she witnessed as a child, when her father maintained this faith as he left for work every morning to inhale the dust.

As the standing-room-only crowd began to fill the back of the church near the opening brass doors, Antonio slipped into the crowd and disappeared towards the main altar. In the background, the Latin *Ave Maria* hymn filled the chamber and echoed throughout the Basilica of the Immaculate Conception.

The Chairwoman Confronts Antonio

The Chairwoman could not stop thinking of the encounter with Antonio at the Basilica. She was moved by his deep beliefs and wondered where his convictions originated. How could she run into him again? She had researched his background and knew he was a trained professional Latin dancer.

The next Friday she decided to try to find Antonio. She thought maybe the tango, salsa, and bachata clubs would be the obvious hangouts for this special agent. She took a chance and visited "La Pachanga," a Mexican music club that played the polka-favorite *rancheros* and *corridos* from northern Mexico. That night the live band was playing the Mexican Cumbia, the genre with its persistent beat of the drum on the upbeats, accompanied by an accordion. The bright ceiling lights of green, blue and red accompanied the rhythm of the vivid Latin sound.

As she arrived, what caught the Chairwoman's eye was the very close bonding of the couples dancing to the Cumbia music. The woman's right arm was slung around the man's back side of his neck, the left hand on the man's waist belt. As the couples swung at a very fast pace, it appeared that the women were holding on for dear life. The Chairwoman thought to herself, *looks like a bull ride at the National Western Stock Show.*

Here, vaqueros wore white and black hats, work blue-jeans, lariat shirts, thick belts with silver belt buckles. and *bota* — boots from the northern Mexican state of Chihuahua. The women wore polyester dresses and skirts that clung to their bodies.

She was not surprised when she walked in and found none other than Antonio, dancing — *tirando chanclas*, which they called dancing to Spanish music. He was dressed in simple Wrangler blue jeans, a wide, tan leather belt with a champion National Western Bull Riding buckle, a tan Stetson hat, and black boots with a Justin logo emblem. His white, long-sleeve shirt contoured his broad shoulders and slim waist, and he wasted no time *tirando chanclas* in perfect step with a lovely dark-haired *Mexicana*, cruising on his broad shoulder. The Chairwoman walked down the aisle closer to the dance floor and caught the attention of Antonio as he finished his dance with *una bonita* — a pretty little thing.

The Chairwoman looked intently at this man with her hazel-green eyes. She wore a tight-fitting, light blue, one-piece dress over her shapely and well-kept figure.

Antonio thought to himself, *What an easy pickup, typically for country, but this evening, for faith.*

He called to her loudly over the music, "No confession booth?"

"I came to see you, to talk to you," the Chairwoman shouted back.

"You found me in a Mexican club. Did they ask you for legal papers when you entered?" Antonio grinned at his spontaneous quip.

As they walked up the aisle to the top platform of the club, the Chairwoman looked keenly at Antonio and said, "I need to speak with you."

Antonio mused, *I have placed countless women as moles, inform-ants, and lookouts, but never one as a head of a major political party.*

He ribbed her, "More judgment on my church attendance?"

"No, I want to understand your point on faith. Can we walk outside?"

They went outside the club, where the lines of *vaqueros* and *caballeras* excitedly buzzed as they waited patiently to gain entrance to dance a Mexican polka. Women were dressed in bright-colored dresses with high pumps and dark net stockings, wearing red lipstick, and earrings that hung to their shoulders. This did not provide the serenity that the Chairwoman sought, a place where she could discuss something near to her soul.

She looked around. "Is there somewhere we can talk quietly?"

At this point Antonio could not tell if the Chairwoman wanted *him* or genuinely wanted to talk about her faith. After a few seconds he took a chance and said, "I don't live that far away. Follow my car, and we can meet at my home."

She agreed to follow him, and as she got into her blue Mercedes-Benz, she told herself, *I need to get close to him to understand him, to understand his faith.*

La Tribunal and the Moral Dilemma

As the Chairwoman followed Antonio into his home, she was struck by the original art, the warmth and serenity as they sat apart in the front room. Hung on the walls were art pieces of the Alhambra in

Granada, a Native American quill rug, and a solo portrait of a genu-flecting Cesar Chavez, all of which provided a broader understanding of Antonio than what the Chairwoman had expected. Before Antonio could say anything, the Chairwoman spoke, "I am not here to be conquered by you. I don't need your love; I'm not a mole or an inform-ant or someone you flip to your side of the Lord. I am here for one reason. I am here to understand your faith."

Antonio, completely taken aback by this woman, thought, *Qué cara tiene esta — What face-boldness this woman has.* Out loud he asked, "You want to explore your faith? Most Americans lack real faith, as if you do not know yourselves. You're here for your father."

"How do you know this?" she asked, astonished.

Antonio stared at her with his serious, brown eyes and let her have it. "You know he passed to his other life, thinking of you, specifically you, because he had so much love for you. Yet you were too busy working in Denver to understand how much he suffered."

The Chairwoman hesitated for a long moment before she could admit the truth. "I know this. Americans move away from their parents to avoid dealing with the suffering of their past and their own past transgressions. I don't know why."

"This is why you do not know yourselves. When your people arrived, they ran over and ostracized the Native American cultures; you never learned a thing from them. Now you do not know your-selves — always leaving your past behind, just as you left your father behind. Now it has caught up with you. Your soul has no home in these lands," Antonio explained.

The Chairwoman looked defeated; her brash and bold American style wore no shine. She glanced down and said, "There is more; I want to understand faith."

"You want faith, yet you have not had a life of sacrifice, as did your father in the mines in Pennsylvania. Yes, I did my research on you," Antonio replied.

"Is that what it takes to gain faith? To live a life of sacrifice of near death?

"No, it takes a respect for life. Respect for those who came before you and to understand how and why they came before you. This you have not done."

Antonio had earlier moved *La Tribunal* — the Bench to the lonely solarium room. There, standing in the middle of the glass windows, it looked special with the moonlight glancing upon its worn pine *facia* and the brown antique nail heads that contrasted the worn cross cuts. Made of simple pinewood with four legs, it was no more than three foot in form.

"Do you want to make the journey to faith, to understand the journey of your father? There is but one way, usually reserved for the ready of spirit, due to the hardship it brings to the soul."

"What is that?" the Chairwoman nervously asked.

"*La Tribunal* — the Bench judgment by Tribunal. The Ladino *Hermano Penitentes* used this bench to bare their soul to the Lord and ask for relief from this life of repression from the Christians. Sweat and tears have poured onto the face of the Bench, where men cried, moaned and trembled as the faith poured out from them, begging for liberation. Here, they ask for the Messiah to arrive to provide the liberation they have anticipated. It is here that *La Tribunal* of the Lord attends to their pleas."

Antonio then asked the Chairwoman to follow him through the portal archway to the solarium, where he pointed to the lonely bench that sat in the middle of the room.

"There it is. If you want to know your faith, you must kneel and place the edge of your elbows and forearms on the *fascia* of the bench. This is typically for the toughest of men. The journey will take you forth to whatever that may hold. The Higher Being God — the Creator — is present there."

Antonio continued to explain, "The Bench is called *La Tribunal* — a Tribunal of collective thoughts that examines one's life by the

Consciousness of the Higher Being God, the Creator. The Tribunal carefully evaluates a person's conscience on the basis of his consciousness. Not often would anticreation values dare to enter this collective conscious space, but you are seeking answers."

"Will I be safe?" she asked hesitantly.

"No, this is a journey to the real faith. Your father knew of contrition and sacrifice; you know that your policies now only support nasty, self-indulgent people. I caution you, though. If you take this journey, you will feel and see your real faith. You will never be the same," Antonio strongly forewarned.

The Chairwoman took a deep breath, removed her heels and walked through the archway into the solarium. The warm flow from the Saltillo tiles and the welcoming walls provided her comfort as she approached the bench. As she knelt down and placed her elbows and forearms upon the rough *fascia* of Earth's wood, emotion swelled from her soul, and she sensed a collective thought that swirled in her consciousness. She wondered to herself, *Is this faith?*

Then clarity appeared as her father, aboard the elevator that descended into the mine. She saw a glaze upon his face, as he calmly and comfortably prayed, not for his safety, but for liberation — *just* as Antonio explained. Liberation would remove him from the danger of this sacrificial life he led. Liberation is the clear connection and acceptance of one's life by the Higher Being God. The swirl in her head returned; the calmness disappeared to a dull sensation, as if a mirror of her life had appeared before her.

Perspiration of sweat and tears fell upon the fascia of the bench. *La Tribunal* realized that the consciousness of the person on the bench was that of a person who had repressed people of faith. Her body began to quiver, her eyes wore a stone stare, her lips began to turn gray. Then clarity returned to the Chairwoman. The true ending of her father's life appeared; her father was not happy with what she did with her life. He was not proud of her policies, which repressed the faithful, and she was not with him at the end of his life. Further, she sensed the appearance of the Messiah.

When Antonio saw her sobbing, he walked over to her, placed his hand on her shoulder and said, "That's enough *hita.*"

The Chairwoman lifted her head and composed herself. She then knew she would never have the faith of grace to join her father. She asked, "How long have I been on the bench?"

Antonio answered, "About 45 minutes. Yet only a few seconds for the Tribunal of the Higher Being God."

The Chairwoman stood up and waddled to the side of the solarium, where she sat down in a chair. She inhaled, then slowly exhaled, before beginning to speak. "I realize my politics have placed limits that may prohibit my joining my father in the afterlife. I may not even get into heaven. My question is, is there any way to avoid this?"

Antonio looked at her and said, "Not to my knowledge." He then asked, "Did you ever stop and think to yourself that your liberal views came without a price to pay?"

"I go to church, I attend Mass, yet I really never thought my politics would bring the Messiah," she answered. "When the Messiah arrives, I understand now that Demos and the large institutions will battle the Messiah. How is this so?"

"You still don't get it." Antonio stated in disbelief. "Your balanced political approach to repress Creation with abortions, synthetic children and adults, birth control of all sorts, laws not to protect families but rather individual needs has caught up to you."

"It happened before. At the beginning of the age of Pisces, the repressed Judaic people requested the coming of the Messiah to liberate them from Romans and non-access to the heavens, and that was Jesus of Nazareth. Now at the beginning of the age of Aquarius, your politics have repressed the persons of faith, and you have repressed liberty. The Messiah has been summoned." Antonio looked at her calmly, "Is it worth it for you, and your liberal agenda?"

"There must be a way to stop this," she said in a dramatic fashion. "Can't you speak to someone, and . . . and tell them to change the course of the action. I did not know, many of us liberals did not know this could happen."

"You did know. You ignored biblical teachings and customs. Your father knew, but you ignored his positions and values. Don't play innocent; your entire party could not care less. You are unable to change this society's politics now," Antonio explained.

The Chairwoman began to weep, her tears flowing down her reddened face. "I didn't know. If I had, I would have steered my party on a different course."

"You women amaze me. Soon as it gets tough, the tears appear, expecting empathy. Do you even realize what you have brought upon society? You have crossed a line of Creation," Antonio said with added concern. "Many persons of faith have been repressed and now will continue to be repressed, especially the working faithful. The difference is now you know there is a price to be paid and it carries a huge price."

"We didn't mean to," she said meekly.

"It's called greed. Power, money, votes. I don't think your type is naïve, nor are you. Many, like you, carry little real faith, so you wouldn't care to have the insight to see this coming, anyhow."

The Chairwoman said, "I don't see the big picture in all of this."

"Faith is the common denominator that overcomes repression," Antonio explained. "This is not a game. Jesus of Nazareth was the Lamb of God, a *turn-the-other-cheek* Messiah. The Higher Being God understands what is required for the people of faith to survive. The next Messiah will be of battle and can take on the large institutions and their allies. Do you not understand the enormity of what you have awakened?"

"Why does this have to happen?" she said pleadingly.

"Typically, when an entity comes to power, they make a mistake, like the Romans with their fixed citizenship status, the Communists with their rigid class structure, the Nazis with their hatred and concentration camps for the Jew. Demos have applied their liberal social values, and the big picture is that these values are not honest and repress the people of faith. Your balanced anticreation politics will impede Creation, using the money from large institutions that protect nasty individual needs, and this will squelch faith and creation from existing. It is not that you don't see this big picture; you do not want to see the repression you have created. Your values have set in motion the coming of the Messiah. He has been called, for you have repressed Creation, and this will be played out!" Antonio spoke with an uncanny authority.

The Chairwoman looked flatly at Antonio. Her sobs lessened as she gathered her breath and said, "My whole life I wanted my father's respect, but I never felt I earned it; now I understand why." Having gathered her composure, she stood up and passed through the portal doorway of the solarium. Behind her, the bench was still warm and moist from her contrite presence.

She let herself out through the front door and moved quickly to her dark blue Mercedes-Benz, pushed her key pod and got into the car. She still shivered at the knowledge that the Tribunal is a collective thought from a higher consciousness.

Driving away in tears, she reflected, *My whole life's work has evolved to repress the original creation. I did not expect such a moral dilemma. And I will never see my daddy.* Now for the first time in her life, she understood that real faith is the creation of mankind's true liberty.

La Tribuna — The Bench

The Chairwoman Meets with the Subaru Guys

The Chairwoman was profoundly moved by her experience at *La Tribunal*. She was overcome by the ability to see and hear the collective thought of the Higher Being God. It provided the understanding of the delicate nature of Creation and the link to the existence of mankind that she had never pondered before. From *La Tribunal*, she also realized that she could not reverse a lifetime of her work that had culminated in working loopholes in the civil rights laws. Instead of being used as they were intended, the laws would be used by non-ethnic people to advance individual rights of groups that are not repressed.

Maybe this did not matter, she thought, but in her heart she knew better. The white communities never liked the civil rights laws, she rationalized. They are not overly religious and will just have to deal with the Messiah upon his or her arrival if that were to happen. She thought to herself, *Is it a coincidence that the women's movement of the past 30 years and the technology that provides abortions, birth control, the creation of synthetic children and body parts arrived at the same time? The women's movement has supported and embraced LGBT rights. I never even cared that another group of persons would be injured by these new acts. I wanted to grow the party, obtain money and votes; that was my job.*

Yet she wondered further, *Will women have to bear the burden of being responsible for the arrival of the Messiah for the many changes that have occurred in society at the impetus of the woman's movement? There have been many acts of brutality of men, but none with the depth and breadth that suppress the working faithful and this Ladino group.*

Yet she was savvy enough to know that life just didn't happen in that calm, orderly fashion. She realized that likely it is time to make payment for the indulgences of the American society.

The Chairwoman called in the henchmen, those Subaru Guys Todger and Champion, to her office to have a talk with them. The Subaru Guys' focus was still fresh from the chase in Northside Denver, pursuing the acquisition of the *cuadernos.*

"I want to talk to you about Antonio and Conjunto," she said as they sat in her downtown office overlooking the 16th Street Mall.

Todger interrupted, "Antonio and Conjunto have to be put down — the people of faith that adhere to Bible Scripture and the Torah like them are from yesterday. Now is our time! We have laws that protect our lifestyle. It doesn't matter where it originated; these laws are for us now."

The Chairwoman thought, *I won't bother mentioning their historical link to the Messiah. The Suburu Guys have no interest in this anyway.*

"I mentioned to you their military backgrounds, didn't I?" the Chairwoman said.

"Yes, that's not something we handle. Find people that can rub these guys out; make them disappear. They're building light rail in these poor areas; stash them in one of those cement casings. We fund most of the DNC operations in what you do here, so it's our money anyway," Todger answered, raising a closed hand with thumb outright to signify the outing of these people of faith.

"I do not have anyone right off the shelf to do that," the Chair-woman said. She could not believe what she heard. "I want you to understand what you are dealing with."

"What do you mean?" Todger asked.

"We have taken poor people's rights and used the civil rights laws of genuine people of color, to give priority rights to your gay community. In doing so, we have awakened the people of faith who will stand against what you have done because it is wrong. They have sources of power that we can never obtain, and they will never stop until they right these wrongs!"

"We don't care; we're getting what we want now. We have you — the women are with us. We can't be stopped!" Subaru Todger exclaimed.

The Chairwoman looked directly at the Subaru guys, "These people of faith have stood up to Nazis, Communists, as well as many extremes, such as dictators and drug lords."

"That's right, those have all been extreme movements with persecution. The LGBT community is now integrated into society, into families. We are in people's homes — in their living rooms. We are on television and they cannot tell who we are. The school children of families will call their parents racists if they are not tolerant. We make the laws now," Todger exclaimed.

The Chairwoman looked down, remembering *La Tribunal*. She finally blurted out, "We have prohibited the Creation of God!"

"Look at you, now! You're not a televangelist, are you? I can't believe you said that. Did you meet up with Antonio and Conjunto, and they gave you some horse shit that God created man and woman in the image of God himself? You just get some heavies to deal with those two and the people of faith." Todger and his boyfriend then stood up and left her office.

The Chairwoman felt personally defeated, but she knew a people of faith movement could not be stopped.

The Subaru Guys

The Subaru guys left the Chairwoman's office and retreated into their smaller office down the hall. Todger signaled that the door be closed, as he peeked out the window shade to ensure no one was within hearing distance. The men sat across from each other in the quiet office room

"In a few years, we won't need the Chairwoman, for our people will chair the DNC for that matter. We will hold those positions," Todger told Champion.

"How is that?"

"She likes to tell men what to do, we kissed that woman's ass. She thought women possessed the position and power, but it is our resources, Gay men and women in power that control the Party," Todger explained.

"How is that possible?"

"Do you know how many married men are gay? You would be surprised. Civil Rights protected the LGBT community. The real ethnic minority's talk is really just lip service. You don't see people of color in management given windows to succeed. We will piggyback what the white women have done; women were given opportunity. Listen, we are loud and we'll sue anyone who denies our Civil Rights. One thing, for sure, white people fear is losing their jobs, so they will look the other way."

"Where does the LGBT community end up?" Champion asked.

"We are the new norm. Federal laws protect us. The constitution will protect us. We will hold public office. You'll see, we'll have our own separate bathrooms in public facilities," Todger explained. "We already control the schools. Next is special educational leadership for LGBT in high schools and then recruiting those students for our purposes."

"But I wasn't gay until three years ago. You were married with kids. How is this to sustain itself?" Champion asked.

"All that doesn't matter." Todger stood up and said.

"Where is the integrity in all of this? You don't really like women. You said, yourself, they were phonies, insecure, greedy, and now you work so closely with them? Champion snapped back.

"All that doesn't matter! Todger raised his hands in frustration.

"At a certain point with our political muscle, we will remove the tax free status of these religious organizations from all these churches. All their properties will be forced to sell, for they have limited income, and then they will lose their power base. Ever notice that Christians act like paupers, always sharing used clothing and food banks with can foods. Such a terrible sight! Ohh!" Todger's face twisted like a squeezed lemon.

"Antonio and Conjunto, they don't fear"? Champion asked.

"They don't have good jobs — no titles, no positions," Todger said as he lifted his closed hand with his thumb out to illustrate they are out of the main stream. "But they have faith, and that is a concern. They must not have a lot of Demo friends. They will turn their backs on them anyway," Todger explained.

"What about the Republicans?" Champion asked.

"They aren't going to support people of color. The *cuardernos*, a Judaic work. They will think this to be un-Christian, and un-American. As they say, 'We got this'," Todger said as he double high-fived Champion. "But we;re not out of the woods yet. Those *Cuardernos* we tried to nab, we don't understand that. The Chairwoman thought those to be a big thing. Did she mentioned the Messiah? I don't see what the big deal is; we already had one, apparently."

CHAPTER 7

The Twin Sun

**2012 in the home of Antonio
Denver, Colorado**

Antonio's *Alabado* of Credence

Antonio entered the solarium in his home. It was early evening and he could feel the warmth of the Saltillo floors under his feet. He looked at the bench — *La Tribunal*. He knew that the historic deciphered writing would not be welcomed with open arms. He knew many would not accept its origin, and, mostly, he knew that the message of the future would not be accepted by a politically correct society. Antonio realized that modern society possibly had turned its back on historic family values and ethos, and become a society fractured at its core, a society that accepted the tolerance of intolerance. More tragically, this era had become a time when the specific values and written words of the Lord were totally ignored. He walked over to the Tribunal, sat down upon the scarred *fascia* facing south, and began to pen the *Alabado of Credence*.

How are the Christians and Jews to believe me?
An insurance agent, surely a Special Agent they will not believe,
A humble person, I have traveled much, yet nobody knows
Stories and craft I can never mention.

To tell them the Messiah is to come,
Without title or position, what will they believe?
To dream, to reach the unreachable star,
My star, the Portal of Light.

Did they select the right person to share this story?
A defender, a fighter that travels without fear
A person with real faith, a person who will walk the walk
Yet who cannot be seen.

Yet this Modern Society was wounded.
The ego of the genders provided no love.
Opportunity and selfishness provided no love
How would the "me" provide love?

The story carried in a cryptic play
Shared at the dawning of the new age.
Is modern society unable to discern this story?
Yet this how the stories of the Lord are shared.

Las Seraditas — Sephardim carry the inalienable Right,
Conceal the right of Redemption.
The arrival of the age of Aquarius
Would bring forward the Messiah.
Will this story be believed?

This Power and Repression cannot be defeated by a mortal being.
You asked that the Ladino people endure this life of
    Spiritual Slavery.
The people of faith live repressed by these policies.
Sweet Lord, deliver us from repression and evil
Lord, I ask that you bring forward the Messiah

Antonio then knelt upon the tiles and pressed his elbows to the
flat fascia of the bench, and he could immediately feel the presence
of the Higher Being God. This overwhelming presence drew his
mind and soul into an area of calm assessment. The Higher Being
God could immediately sense Antonio's weakness of spirit and his
understanding of the true purpose of the notebooks.

Then, his uncertainty and pause of his role as messenger turned into clarity and purpose. He felt the strength of the backbone of the Higher Being God. His loneliness of cause turned into the focus and strength and knowledge of the Higher Being God. Antonio lifted his head and knew, regardless of what others might think or say or what actions they might take against him, his work would be supported by the Lord. He knew then to go forward without fear.

The 2012 New Year and the Age of Aquarius
Union Station, Downtown Denver, Colorado

The end of the year 2012 completed the astrological age of Pisces. It began at the birth of Jesus of Nazareth as the Pisces constellation crossed the celestial equator and continued these past 2,012 years. When this constellation age ended, a new reign began — Aquarius — identified as the symbolic image of a woman pouring water from a jug high in the sky. It is also representative of the empowerment of women obtaining higher positions in their worldly lives during the second millennium.

Under the fireworks and celebration of this New Year at the downtown Denver Union Station, the celebrants had no idea of the significance and transformation of this new age. The mystical Judaic background of the Kaballah had provided Antonio the unique knowledge of the astrological phenomena that was arriving and its impact upon society. However, the Chairwoman and the many women of her generation had no idea that their progressive, liberal views would influence the very existence of herself, her family and her gender in this new age of Aquarius.

Standing in front of Union Station, the Chairwoman, the Subaru Guys and her staff were all gathered, their breath exhaling like fog, as they waited for the countdown for the New Year. Antonio and

Conjunto arrived and approached the jubilation, catching the eye of the Chairwoman. She wondered, *How did they know I would be here? Am I already under surveillance?*

Antonio was dressed in a brown bomber jacket with a fur white lapel, and blue corduroy jeans. Conjunto wore blue jeans, and a long jacket down to his boot tops, similar to the cold weather coats worn in the old western movies.

As the two neared the Chairwoman, she recognized the insignia upon Antonio's left shoulder on the bomber jacket: 721st Com Squad Unit-NORAD. Her research never revealed anything about a Com Squad unit.

"What brings you here?" she asked Antonio.

"Just here to see the beginning of the new age," Antonio answered.

The Chairwoman now knew to listen carefully to his words, though she had no idea what he was talking about, and then she remembered *La Tribunal.* She asked him, "Does this have anything to do with my journey?"

Antonio looked down and pondered a bit, then his eyes awoke and he said, "Your journey to sense Creation provided you with insight of your future."

Subaru Todger butted in, "Are you here to harass us? You know I will call the cops."

Conjunto opened his long coat, stepped forward at the Subaru guys and said, "Not today ese. Just observing." The clock on Union Station arrived at 12:00 midnight, and the jubilation began as party-goers started dancing and blowing horns all around with hugs in abundance. Yet no one had any idea that the age of Aquarius had just begun.

As the jubilants returned to Democratic Party headquarters, the Chairwoman went into to her office, closed her door and began to ponder her experience on the *La Trubunal. I saw and felt the presence of the creator, and its existence is incompatible with my party's politics.*

Then she began to wonder about the 721st Com Squad insignia on Antonio's jacket, *Was he an Air Force cadet or a pilot? And what did he have to do with NORAD — the North American Aerospace Defense Command in Colorado Springs?*

By now, Antonio and Conjunto had slipped away, walked to the Impala and got into the car.

Conjunto asked Antonio, "Who are those Subaru Guys?"

"Todger is a white, entitled staff member, private schools with an elite life, was married and had children. The name Todger is an old English name; it means penis or dick."

Conjunto laughed something silly, his shoulders bopping up and down like a lowrider bounce contest. Then he asked about "the other one."

"Subaru Champion, well, there is no story other than he changed his name to Champion from Matthew because he did not like his Christian name. He is not a champion of anything," Antonio explained.

"Can we go some place to talk? It's late out," Conjunto asked.

"Yeah, get on Colfax and drive east. We can go to Pete's Central Café. It's open 24 hours a day, 365 days a year," Antonio said. They arrived at the café, where the underside of Denver's urban population was drawn to its unique character of a communal night eatery. Not one person was dressed the same. Each had different hairdos, funky colored coats of leather, and came from every imaginable walk of life. Everyone was always welcome there. The owners were Greek, the cooks were Mexicans, and the waitresses were white women. Antonio and Conjunto sat down in a skinny booth for two. The silver metal railings gave way to the black pleather seats, as the two men looked at their ketchup-stained menus.

The waitress appeared tired in her wilted clothes and politely asked, "What will you boys be having this New Year's morning?" Antonio ordered his favorite, "I would like chicken fried steak with the white sauce, a side of your home fries and water with lemon, *por favor.* Oh, and a side of your green chile. You still got your Mexicano cooks, I see."

Conjunto looked at her, "Let's go with your Americano here: two eggs over medium, some of those home fries, a large Coke and wheat toast, to be healthy," he said as he smiled at her and snuggled warmly against the comfortable pleather booth.

But Conjunto was a bit nervous because he wanted to share an in-depth conversation with Antonio. He thought he had earned more information from him by running with him in some tight spots without being pinched by las Chotas, el PoPo, the police. "I see, you roll with the working class here at this place," he finally said.

"Well, not all of them work," Antonio chuckled.

"Let me talk with you, Antonio. When the Spanish first arrived in the mid 1500's, the Acoma people were forced to conceal and pre-serve our religious and dance ceremonies in secret underground kivas"

"I am familiar with the preservation of your culture," Antonio told him.

"Your *cuadernos* were hidden in these kivas in the Acoma village," Conjunto said matter-of- factly.

Antonio was taken aback and said, "They preserved the *cuadernos* in the kivas? This I did not know. I wondered how such an old story had been preserved."

The food arrived, and the hungry men were surprised by the large portions offered to them. The two used their spoons to empty the bowl of green chile atop their potatoes and began to eat.

"This means there was a long established relationship between your *Ladino Hermanos* and our elders. I wonder if they shared stories of the cosmos?" Antonio asked with genuine curiosity.

"I realize you have knowledge, but so do I, and so does my Acoma tribe."

"European societies never once paid any attention to the astro-logical studies of existing Native American cultures; they just rolled over them," Antonio explained something Conjunto was all too familiar with.

"We preserved and hid our knowledge in the secret underground kivas. My tribe has equipped me to share some of the knowledge of the sun. We want to know what depth of knowledge your Ladino mystics know of this subject," Conjunto explained.

"Hmm, I was wondering why you were sent. Now this comes full circle," Antonio observed as the courteous waitress brought two cups of black coffee to the table. He continued, "In the late 1500s, when the Ladino soldiers and families first arrived to an Acoma village, as well with all the other villages, we sought out either your medicine men or sacred dancers. Most of the time, they were one and the same. We identified them and made the effort to speak with them privately soon after."

"How were you able to do this at such a confusing time period?" asked Conjunto.

"Initially, at the onset of establishing the Christian faith in the pueblo, some of the priests were educated Ladinos who spoke Tewa. He was able to calmly communicate with your sacred people. A relationship was established, a relationship of faith in a higher spirit and the understanding of the power of the sun and its travel patterns," Antonio explained.

"An understanding took place?" Conjunto asked.

"Yes, your sacred dance and knowledge of the sun was to be preserved and concealed in the underground secret kivas," Antonio explained.

"Do you know where the sacred kivas exist? Tell me what they look like," Conjunto probed to verify Antonio's knowledge.

"Typically this sacred site was viewed plainly in a vacant meadow," Antonio said. "You do not see any sign of pathways, grass or weeds grown in plain sight, except a lid made of maybe plywood is lifted into what looks like a dark hole. This is your kiva, a sacred site preserved for the most spiritual persons of your tribe. The medicine men would have you follow them to the entry. You must take a wooden ladder down into the ground. At first it seems you are entering a dark hole, but as you reach ground, you realize that you have entered a large cavern."

"What is in the cavern?" Conjunto asked.

"Feathers of various sizes and shapes. Bowls filled with burned aftermath of various herbs. Blankets of various sizes, colors and shapes cover the dirt floors and dirt — pounded chairs. The air is dense and cool. Only when candles are lit can you see any of these objects in the cavern," Antonio explained.

"Did these men dance for you?" Conjunto asked.

"No," answered Antonio.

"That is right. They would not have danced the sacred dances of the sun and astrology for you or for your people," Conjunto confirmed.

"I have a question for you. Your knowledge of the sun patterns. Where did this come from?" Antonio tested Conjunto's understanding.

"It did not come from us originally. It came to us from the Hopi tribe, a distant cousin. Both Acoma and Hopi tribes are related to the Anasazi tribe of Chaco Canyon," Conjunto explained.

"That is correct," Antonio confirmed, also verifying Conjuto's knowledge.

Both Antonio and Conjunto were at a tipping point; both wanted to verify the other's knowledge of the sun without compromising their own knowledge.

"Tell me," Conjunto asked, "What do you call the sun?"

"We call this sun, *el Sol*."

"What do you mean *this sun*? Conjunto asked, again testing Antonio's detailed sacred knowledge.

Antonio sipped his coffee and looked around a bit. He knew he had tipped his hand and realized that Conjunto was aware of the history of the sun.

"The sun you see in the sky has a twin, a sun that our current sun is patterned after," Antonio explained.

"Yes, the twin was much older and provided the existence for our current Father Sun to be present," Conjunto explained. "The First Sun was four times larger than our current sun. Upon its implosion, it gave life to our present sun and the Milky Way constellation."

Both men looked at each other in amazement; they both possessed this sacred knowledge. They smiled at each other and shook hands across the table at, of all places, Pete's Café in downtown Denver. *Sacred knowledge can be shared anywhere*, they both thought.

"Boy, do I feel relieved! We each thought we were the only ones that were aware of this sacred awareness," Antonio said with a smile.

"What did your sacred writers call this sun?" Conjunto asked.

"It was called *Semano*. It comes from the Ladino origin, actually a Turkish word." A relieved Antonio was happy to finally share with another kindred spirit community.

"We called the old sun the First Sun. This was watched by the Sun Watcher, an early historic astronomer within our tribe, who studied the movement of this star. When the sun rose to a certain point, he informed both the sun clan and kiva societies that a specific dance ceremony was to take place," Conjunto explained. "But why is the First Sun of such importance now?"

"The word *semano* is revealed in the play. That is in the *cuaderno*."

"Why is the *cuaderno* revealing the *semano* now?" Conjunto said, surprised.

"I am not ready to share the entire story with you today, but stay close and you will see why," Antonio stated with caution. "I understand now why your Sun Watcher would preserve the sacred knowledge of the sun in a cryptic dance. The ancient knowledge of the sun sheds an understanding of the cosmos. The secrecy makes sense to me now."

"Tell me, where does all of this wisdom originate?" Conjunto asked impatiently. "My tribe really wants to know where this intuitiveness comes from."

CHAPTER 8

The Conscious Directive of the Portal of Light

The Technology of the Portal of Light

1733, New Mexico Territory
Chupadero, NM
In the home of Pedro with Jila and the Hermitaño

The Hermitaño had arrived at an adobe home in the rugged and arid terrain in the New Mexico territory in the small village of Chupadero. The dry and hilly landscape was the crossroad between the Rocky Mountains ridgeway and the dry desert sands of this realm. This unique landscape knitted together the static knowledge of the Christian faith with the esoteric insight of the cosmic awareness known by the hidden Ladino community of this area.

The home of Pedro on the periphery looked like every other house in the adobe enclave, yet the interior provided clues as to the knowledge of the ancient Judaic mystics: the southern facing windows and shutters, the menorah and the tall candelabrum holders in the corner, the Jewish cross hung upon the wall, the *santo* — saint of St. Esther in the kitchen.

Jila was visiting Pedro. At the knock on the door, she opened it to find the Hermitaño dressed in vaquero clothing. She asked him to come in and have a seat. All three sat quietly at the table, looking outside at the splendor of the mountains.

The Hermitaño accompanied the Portal of Light on the journey from *Semano*, the original heaven for both the Judaic mystics and the *Ladino Hermanos*. He arrived to explain the energy matter that comprises the Portal and its purpose.

"How long did the Portal take to arrive from Capricornus?" Jila asked.

"Cosmic travel in the world of Dark Matter typically takes two years, yet with fourth dimension navigation capabilities, the travel time of a few years was compressed into six months," Hermitaño explained.

Cosmic Time is that of a fluid, spatial dimension with infinite generation of movement that interacts well with the particles of dark matter and dark energy. The particle of time is invisible, non-reflective but yet absorbent to act as a gel or coagulant to permit matter to be manipulated into a design.

"This is the formula," Hermitaño said. "Let me write it down for you." Jila found a piece of paper, ink, and pen, and put it on the table for him. In fluid writing, he put down:

Time+Direct Matter+Direct Energy = Conscious Directive

"Time is infinite and without boundaries in fourth dimension. There is no distinction or separation of length, width, or depth as in third dimension, or earthly world. This indicative of sending snail pace hardware craft to distance moons, planets and asteroids is third dimension thinking. A craft or cosmic event that thrusts itself in the regular universal atmosphere encounters natural friction that limits the craft to travel at a limited velocity," Hermitaño explained.

Artist Robert Maestas' 2015 drawing of the Cosmic Tornado

This drawing of a Cosmic Tornado demonstrates how at the bottom right, friction is created as a young star travels in the cosmos. As the explosion cuts through gas clouds and debris in our galaxy, this limits maximum velocity due to a friction trail of orange sparks that appear. This was similar to the Space Shuttle or Apollo Lunar Mission shields of friction as they entered the Earth's atmosphere.

"Understand that the higher dimensions are ancient. They resigned to the fact to survive in the spiritual world, only their organic self existed. The hybrids and synthetics do not exist in the higher dimensions," Hermitano explained.

"The Portal that travels in the atmosphere of Dark Matter and Dark Energy will navigate without friction, using a Plank Propulsion system," Hermitaño said.

"Did the Higher Being God develop this cosmic travel vehicle?" Pedro asked.

"Yes, it took many, many thousands of years for this to be developed," Hermitaño replied.

"Can you tell us about this Plank Propulsion system?" Jila asked.

"Did the Higher Being-God develop this cosmic travel vehicle?" Pedro asked.

"Yes, it took many, many thousands of years for this to be developed," Hermitaño replied.

"The Portal is an invisible transparent membrane with a hollow core and whiplash strands that link on to one another via low lying magnetic small spurs that hold together this transport of travel. These interlocking strands or strings of flowing movement work in conjunction with both Dark and Energy Matter to create a supersonic velocity. It is a flowing and fluid propulsion system of infinite non-resistance energy that is able to travel light years within the cosmic energy fields of space. This is not a cloaking field, but rather a transportation field," Hermitaño said.

"This craft moves at such hyper speed that, to a naked eye, it appears to stop or move in channels," Pedro said.

"You are correct. How do you know this?" Hermitaño asked.

"Our vision of waiting for a sign of the Emmanuel emanates from the thought that the cosmos is an art form. The cosmic universe must be viewed from the fourth dimension, where Time has its own realm, its own velocity, its own way of doing things. It is Time in relation to Space," Pedro said.

"Can human observations observe this channel movement in the fourth dimension? Hermitaño asked to understand the knowledge of the earthly world.

"To view the cosmos in a logical form is the natural weakness of Science, the effort to quantify the invisible — the surreal — the faith is the real art form of the cosmos."
Anthony Garcia, *The Portal of Light*

"Science cannot see consciousness, just as most persons on this earth cannot see or comprehend the concept of '*duende*,' yet we know it exists. This concept is understood as a mysterious force that everyone senses but no philosopher can explain. An earth spirit that assists artists to rise to evocation in their art performance far beyond their natural ability can be visualized, but not quantified," Pedro said.

"You're saying your future scientists that work with matter must look at Dark Matter and Energy as an art form to grasp their principles, or they will be unable to quantify its existence?" Hermitaño asked.

"Yes, the cosmos is an esoteric world. To view the cosmos in a logical form is the natural weakness of science, the effort to quantify the invisible — the surreal — the faith is the real art form of the cosmos. Time is a fluid state in the cosmos, not a static form that can be quantified. The concept we need to grasp is the fluidity of Time in relation to Space itself," Pedro said.

"Give me an example of Time in relation to space itself." Hermitano wondered how this technology-less society was aware of this advanced travel concepts.

"Comprehend the movement of a chord from a stringed instrument within the framework of the concept 'Duende'. The strumming movement of a chord possesses the capabilities of being able to propel a craft at light-speed level. This is a mysterious art form that man senses but cannot quantify the origin of its power. Plank propulsion is the movement of a cord, in a whiplash movement. To the naked eye, plank is invisible, yet the movement creates an immense energy propulsion of the craft," Pedro explained.

Hermitaño asked, "Where does this knowledge of plank propulsion come from?"

"Our knowledge comes from the tradition given to us by mystics and the Kabbalah. In the play, *Jornade de Exódo*, the concepts of velocity and distance to the *Semano* or Heaven were concealed within the writing of the play. This originated from the ancestry of the original Judaic mystics and later the Kabbalists," Jila explained.

"Tell me of the persons who wrote the play. Did they possess much knowledge of Judaic history?" Hermitaño asked.

"The play was written anonymously, influenced by Kabbalist Moshe Cordoviero, who wrote the mystical classic "Pardes Rimonim" (Garden of Pomegranates) in 1548," Jila said.

"They were Kabbalists?" Hermitano queried knowingly.

"There is influence in the play from what is called Cabbalists with a "C." This group fled to New Spain with a philosophy to harmonize the Kabbalah with Christianity. A new purpose was to interconnect the first three sepheroths of the Trinity, Father, Son, and Holy Ghost with the legacy of the Kabbalah," Pedro explained.

"Were they Kabbalists?" the Hermitaño asked.

"Not in the purist form since they would have been prohibited from this practice in New Spain. This community used the knowledge of the Kabblah for concealment and survival," Jila said. "The community used the 'Pardes' techniques to conceal themselves, much like the Higher Being God hides his/her technology. Maybe someday in the future, the techniques to reveal the real spiritual power will be disclosed."

"This ability to conceal themselves and their knowledge is similar to how the Higher Being God functions. The incredible work of creation exists in the Dark Matter, yet most are unable to view the force; still, you know it performs," Hermitaño declared as one who carried secrets from afar.

The Future

"Your astrophysicists will never completely comprehend the cosmic world. Hard science will not provide the logical solutions that they will depend upon to make sense of an esoteric world," Hermitaño said.

"Will they be able to peel back the knowledge that is concealed by the Higher Being God? Like venture into the fourth dimension? Create a travel craft comprised of Dark Matter and Energy or go behind the dark curtain?" Pedro asked.

"Only if they respect the universal laws of the spirituality expected by the Higher Being God. Your society has the laws of the Torah and the Old Testament. The Higher Being God will only respect those that self-created in its image. Self-creating in the Higher Being God's orientation is essential to be able to function in this ambiance, or the knowledge will never be shared," Hermitaño explained.

"Will *Flaton* — Foul experiences be imposed for those who do not respect this law?" Jila asked.

"Yes, that is how it works. Some societies just keep shoving their perspective that is contrary to why mankind was created by the Higher Being God. They are never granted the knowledge and are never able to live within the fourth dimension. Maybe it is better that some societies do not spend their precious cosmic or travel resources in a place where they will not be able to exist," Hermitaño said.

"This would mean that third dimension technology, friction craft, snail velocity craft, and limited capacity astrophysics would be the only technology available to these societies. The jump to a next-level technology will not be available to societies that do not live the word of the Lord," Jila observed.

"Yes, these societies will not survive in the higher-level dimensions. They will not be granted the capacity to build a Cosmic Adaptor or be able to create a craft such as the Portal of Light. This is how you will know your society has evolved to be a higher dimension level," Hermitaño said.

"What would happen to Earth itself? Pedro asked.

"Earth's very existence will be challenged. The third level technology is the dependence upon unclean fossil fuel mechanization for cosmic travel. At some point the atmosphere itself will be challenged by this unclean energy dependence. When a society does not make the correct decisions to exist in a future world, it will not be granted access to fourth dimensional technology. That society will be sending spacecraft to look for a new Earth to move their most important people and families to, for they know they have destroyed their own planet. This has happened on numerous occasions," the Hermitaño said.

"This is important to know. How is this to be avoided?" Pedro asked.

"Understand that the higher dimensions are ancient. They resigned to the fact to ascend and survive that the spiritual world, only their organic self-existed. The hybrids and synthetics do not exist in higher dimensions," the Hermitaño explained.

"Many societies believe man and woman derived from the primate-monkey and do not believe creation by a Higher Being God. What do you think of this? Jila asked

"Just camouflage and misdirection so that the dark world is not revealed. The Higher Being God is very good at not revealing secrets," the Hermitaño said.

"The spiritual world is an organic natural world. The technology of faith is what determines advanced knowledge to exist in the fourth dimension, the ability to comprehension that the hyper travel craft Portal is constructed via the conscious directive by the Higher Being God," Hermitaño said.

"When will humans be able control both Dark Energy and Dark Matter?" Jila asked.

"This will come with the acceptance and understanding of how the Portal of Light was able to travel and attend the birth of the Emmanuel. Then there will an understanding of how matter functions," The Hermitaño explained.

In the future, humans may be able to enter a time frame that will be able to control both Dark Energy and Dark Matter. Slowing peeling back the concealed knowledge of God and the possible discovery of scientific know how will permit galactic travel, Plank Propulsion and Gravity Management with Dark Matter technology will be ascertained. The more advanced civilizations are in alignment with the word of their Lord and will be able to manage Conscious Management of Gravity and Time Travel.

CHAPTER 9

The Chairwoman's
One Question

Location: St. Catherine's Church
Denver, Colorado
Time: Early January, 2012

The profound depth of her experience on the Bench — *La Tribunal* left the Chairwoman both emotionally and spiritually inspired by the knowledge and purpose of Creation. Never had it been shared with her that spiritual liberty or real freedom was the benefactor of Creation by the Higher Being God itself. *La Tribunal* also shared with her that her dream of joining her father in the afterlife was not a foregone conclusion, as she always assumed. She learned that heaven was reserved for those who foster Creation; the others were to be stuck in an afterlife of dullness, a silence of nothingness, not in one glorious reunion with family.

This led her to re-examine her life of liberal politics, a life that repressed both people of faith and those who maintained the existence of Creation. She thought to herself, *The people of my party had no idea that true liberty was a surviving factor from the Creator and that the Messiah has been requested to arrive.* She now understood that the people of faith had aligned themselves with the Messiah and her leadership of the liberal politics had led them to do this. Still, she wondered, *Is it too late to change the direction of the ship? Can I inform party leaders of this new insight and ask them to stop the course that is impeding Creation?*

Finally, the Chairwoman realized that it was too late to make any changes to the liberal politics and the trajectory of the party's policies in the future. As a Sacrament Catholic, she never really understood the purpose of sacraments nor the effect her party's policies had in bringing the wrath of the divine Creator upon them. She now finally understood the entire picture, yet there was nothing she could do to prevent the inevitable clash between the Messiah and her liberal politics.

The *cuadernos* brought forward the start of the arrival of the Messiah by the request of the Ladino people of faith who were all too familiar with repression. The people of faith will inherit the Earth with the arrival of the Messiah, standing firm against her liberal politics in the age of Aquarius.

What she did not see was that she and her party followers were so full of themselves that they followed the path of a frequent story of an American tragedy, that is, to ignore the values and customs that existed prior to their arrival. Just as the customs and values of Native Americans were completely ignored, the DNC's liberal policies repressed the family values and customs that had initially created her party.

The Chairwoman unceremoniously decided to quietly change her personal point of view on moral issues, but decided not to share her knowledge with DNC party leaders and to maintain her position as chairwoman. Practical maybe, but keeping in fashion with DNC members, for their title and position were more important than family values or the people of faith.

Yet the Chairwoman felt that she needed more insight and knowledge, so she decided to go visit Father Martin at St. Catherine's. She asked the Subaru Guys to go with her on this cold and snowy evening for the evening Mass.

Antonio called Conjunto, who was in town visiting Enselmo, and asked his friend once again to go with him to confront the Subaru

Guys. Antonio had a hunch what the Chairwoman's next move would be, and Enselmo overheard Conjunto on the phone.

All parties met at St. Catherine's, where a light crowd had gathered on a Tuesday evening. Father Martin had come to the end of the Mass and was about to give his final blessing with "May Almighty God Bless You, the Father . . . the Son and" when at that moment he saw to his left a woman walking up toward the altar, towards the pulpit and the microphone. It was the Chairwoman! MaryBeth Maddox did one of the greatest "faux pas, Oh no, you didn't" maneuvers in the history of womenhood. She grabbed the microphone during Mass, and spoke loud and clear:

> "As Chairwoman of the DNC, the lives of women have been vastly improved under my tenure. Not always will that be in accord with church teachings. I have recently found out that my actions do have, shall we say, limitations, a cause and effect, and I want everyone to know that I have been enlightened."

The slight crowd stood motionless. Antonio and Conjunto, standing at the back of the church, began to walk towards the altar. Father Martin glanced at his second priest to nudge him out of his shocked and frozen state and motioned for him to unplug the microphone. The Chairwoman and the priest looked at each other, standing across from each other with the altar separating the two entities. Father Martin was well aware of her lofty political status, but at this moment his look could have turned wine into water — the kind that could drown people in.

"Can we talk?" The Chairwoman asked.

The priest, uncertain of her motive and still in front of a stunned congregation, pointed towards the vestibule, which led to a separate chamber that housed a font for the sacred baptismal rituals. All parties began walking toward the separate chamber.

The Chairwoman was surprised to see both Antonio and Conjunto as they neared the baptismal font. When they had gathered to one side of the vestibule, she said, "My, you have impeccable timing. Did you plan this, or are you just lucky?" The Subaru Guys stood motionless next to her.

Father Martin entered last and closed the chamber doors. Then, standing between the two parties, he said, "Nothing like a good showdown." The savvy priest continued, "Let me surmise. On my left we have the liberals, and on my right, the working faithful. What do you want me to do, referee a boxing match?"

The Chairwoman raised her head and boldly interjected, "Father Martin, I have but one question. Do these Ladino faithful have a right to call for the Messiah to come?"

Father Martin looked Antonio square in the eyes. "In my years of servicing the profound faith of those in their darkest hours, my answer is this: The *cuadernos* arrived at the appropriate time in the year 2012, brought forward by the original Judaic peoples of these lands, repressed in spirit for centuries now. Yes, they have the inalienable right to call for a Messiah!"

The Chairwomen and the Subaru Guys stood stunned and silent; they knew this priest had nothing to gain or lose in this drama. To the Chairwoman, it was always about swaying a vote or a measure, to get what she wanted. She knew all her cards were laid on the table, and she had set in motion a spiritual law that never could be stopped. She and the Subaru guys looked down and walked out of the church.

Father Martin looked at Antonio and Conjunto and said, "You finally show your face. I guess it is consistent with so many things in our faith being considered a mystery. Nobody ever believed Jesus of Nazareth would appear, but He did. This story may never gain credence. I expect the liberals and the far right from my faction would never believe this was possible. Yet in all my years of servicing the faith of souls, it is the working faithful that have carried the most honest beliefs." The priest then took one last glance at Antonio and left towards the sacristy.

Enselmo had followed Antonio and Conjunto to St Catherine's and watched the entire event unfold. He was amazed how the authentic honesty of each party and the genuine, objective setting of the church had brought out the truth of all parties in this parley.

Conjunto noticed Enselmo and said, "How did you find us?"

"It is not hard to locate that 1964 blue Impala with the seal of the Acoma Nation on your yellow license plate, now is it?" Enselmo said laughingly. "Quite a showdown tonight! The tranquility of this historic church was surely lifted. Nothing like a good *chingaso* — fight in front of a priest."

"Let me introduce you to Antonio. I think you know of him," Conjunto said as the two shook hands.

"We may know of each other through the Ladino families in New Mexico," Enselmo said.

"That's what I am gathering. Gracias for putting up our friend Conjunto. He is invaluable. His faith in the spirit of the Lord is truly una maravilla — a marvel," Antonio answered.

"Quite a parley with the chairwoman. The real faith had to be shown to her," Enselmo observed. "I wonder if she has learned anything and would now adjust her political philosophies."

"That is the question. Did the Chairwoman and those similar to her grasp real faith? They did not internalize the word of the Lord ever initially and did not understand that the Word of the Lord lives perpetually. They have crossed the line of Creation, and now the proverbial Pandora's box has been opened. They have challenged Creation and will now be met by an equally strong power of the Lord," Antonio explained.

"We must leave before the Chairwoman sends her enforcers to deal with us," Conjunto urged. "*Vamos ahora* — Let's go now!"

CHAPTER 10

Martha Washington's Garden and the Carnation

Washington Park
Denver, Colorado
January 2012

Antonio, Conjunto and Enselmo left the church bewildered and surprised by the turn of events at the historic church. Antonio did not expect the old priest to understand the dynamic underpinnings of faith and conflict in the Ladino community but, then again, that was his industry.

Conjunto led the way to his Impala, parked in front of the church, and nervously said, "Get in, let's get out of here. We may be followed."

Once they were all seated inside, Conjunto started the car. "Move fast, let's take the side streets. The Chairwoman did not seem pleased at what the old priest told her. She could be sending some heavies to follow us." He peered to the side and behind to see if anyone was following them. He decided to take a route past downtown Denver to Speer Boulevard, then south on Downing to head to Washington Park.

"Turn into the Park on Franklin," Antonio said. "I know of a place to lay low." As they turned into Washington Park to ensure they had not been followed, they stopped and parked, but left the headlights on.

Looking out the front window, they were amazed to see, through the headlights, the stunning beauty of a manicured garden surrounded by patches of snow. *El jardín* — the garden was an exact replica of Martha Washington's garden at Mount Vernon in Virginia. Behind the flowering bed of beauty, the moonlight glossed over the waters of Grasmere Lake in the background.

Antonio, Conjunto and Enselmo got out of the Impala to get a better look. The high moon glistened upon an unbelievable sight in the garden — a flock of pink carnations in full bloom on a cold, brisk night in January. The bouquet of deep pink clusters of green-stemmed carnations filled the courtyard.

The sweet scent of clove, vanilla and cinnamon filled the cool night air, and the three men were taken aback by this miraculous event.

Conjunto immediately noticed the genuine spiced aroma of the carnations and reached back into his car to retrieve an orange. He then began a prayer offering with his arms extended in front of his body, as he reverently held out the fruit in thanksgiving for the grace he was witnessing.

Immersed in prayer and reverence, Conjunto made this most high offering of grace and thanks in the name of the Native American community.

Enselmo stared at the long-stem carnations, mystified at the sight of these fresh flowers in a garden surrounded by light snow. He stopped in his tracks and thought, *This is not possible.*

Antonio noticed a gardener working in the late evening hours, dressed in blue jeans, a white long-sleeve shirt, and a wide-brim straw hat, bending at every odd angle, tending the garden. He recognized the figure, the Hermitaño.

Antonio walked over to talk to him. "You appear as a gardener. My family background — farm workers — I get it now." Antonio looked at him closely, "Your lower back must be killing you." He laughed as he remembered the painful essence of farm work.

Hermitaño stood, looked sternly at Antonio and said, "You learned an important lesson tonight — what it takes to defend the Word of the Lord. You must learn to team-build as you have done with Conjunto and Enselmo. It is not easy. You are not the first to go through this, and you will not be the last."

"Tell me, what is this all for? Every time this story is shared, it is met with rejection and ridicule. It feels like I am telling people the sky is falling," Antonio asked.

"Do you think the story that the early Christians told was accepted? Their story was not accepted. They were persecuted for their knowledge. That is why Mother Mary's family and close circle of friends fled. This is the beginning. This is how it works. You were picked because you are strong. It was not going to be easy. Look at your friend Conjunto over there, immersed in prayer and meditation. He may not have the historic depth of knowledge that you have, yet he possesses the deep spirit of faith. And with this I say, *"Hasta la vista* — Until I see you again," the Hermitaño smiled and waved.

Antonio walked back to the Impala and joined Enselmo and Conjunto, who had finished his prayer. They watched as the Hermitaño walked away from the garden toward the pathway to the lake. His shadow mirrored upon the lake as the moonlight traced his disappearing walk into the night air.

"I do have one question," Enselmo asked. "Did you tell anyone of the origin of the alternate story of the night Jesus of Nazareth was born, and who the story came from?

Antonio looked at him with surprise. *How did he have this knowledge?* "Not yet," he said.

"Now would be the right time. You have informed everyone that the Messiah is coming. The *cuadernos* have been shared," Enselmo pointed out.

"Do you think people are ready for this important inheritance of the story?" Antonio asked.

"Tell me about this story. I want to know, too," Conjunto demanded.

Antonio looked down and then up at the stars in the sky. He slowly breathed in and thought to himself, *Sharing this veiled story may forever change the way the cuadernos are looked upon.*

"The story comes from Mother Mary's family. The Portal of Light is what she saw as the Hermano shepherds brought comfort items to the cave and paid homage to the Messiah, the baby Jesus," Antonio slowly shared in a low voice.

"How did this story end up in your hands, Antonio?" Conjunto asked.

"After the death of her son, Mother Mary and their followers fled to Iberia, essentially northern Spain. Later they became the Sephardim; *las Seraditas* they were called," Antonio explained.

"This story has been preserved and has traveled a lengthy journey for it now to appear," Enselmo observed.

"The story and journey of original faith should never stop," Antonio clarified. "The Cross and the Star of David need to unite for the Messiah to arrive. Today the Chairwomen, her supporters are made aware that they have crossed the line of Creation."

Glossary

Antonio: Sleuth, Special Agent and Messenger to decipher and share story of the *Cuaderno* — Notebook.

Conjunto: Native American Penitente from the Cliff reservation in Acoma, New Mexico.

Cuadernos — Notebook: *Jornado de Exódo* play passed down among Ladino families starting in 1733.

Hermitaño: The Time Traveler beginning with voyage of the Portal of Light (1 B.C.) to present day.

Chairwomen: Marybeth Maddox, chairwomen of the Democratic National Committee.

Enselmo: Friend of Conjunto, lives in Denver, Co and is a former Ladino Hermano Penitente.

Father Martin: Priest at St. Catherine parish in northwest Denver, Colorado.

Hermandad: Brotherhood of the Penitents known as Los *Hermanos* Penitentes.

Jila: Original character in *Jornado de Exódo* play, her name is passed down generations by her family.

Ladino: Person, word or reference of the hybrid creation/synthesis of Spanish and Hebrew.

The Portal of Light: Original light that Judaic shepherds followed to greet the birth of the Emmanuel-baby Jesus of Nazareth.

La Trubunal — The Bench: Confessional bench used by Ladino Hermano Penitentes and the subliminal relationship to the Higher Being God.

Alabado "*La Marca* — The Mark": *Alabado* that references the Judaic Mark of the Covenant between God and Mankind. (Joshua 5, Torah).

*Note: All names of characters are fictional.

About the Author

Anthony Garcia is the founder of TwentyFirst Century Investments and Benefits, located in Denver, Colorado. A native Coloradoan with family roots in northern New Mexico, he is in constant contact with the land and people of the 33° Latitude in New Mexico. Garcia has earned a M.S. in Finance, a M.S. Minor in Health Administration from the University of Colorado-Denver and B.S. in Business from the University of Colorado-Boulder.

Garcia is the founder and writer of the website *www.Alabados.com* of which is the original basis and impetus for the writing of his first book, *The Portal of Light*. Garcia listened to Alabados as a child and the lyrics and genre always peaked his interest which began his study of the Alabados. The organic understanding of the Kabbalah and esoteric concepts are innate to Garcia's historical linkage to his family ties to the origin of the Alabados. He enjoys traveling and Latin dance.

Copies of *Portal of Light* can be ordered at *www.ThePortalLight.com*.

Contact Anthony Garcia at:

email: anthony@theportallight.com
Twitter: agtwit12
LinkedIn: xxicent@aol.com
Google: xxicent@aol.com
Facebook: xxicent@aol.com

Made in the USA
San Bernardino, CA
16 July 2017